P9-CFK-973
WHAT HAPPENS NEXT?
Newsroom Nonsense
JESS SMART SMILEY
HOW TO DRAW MR. FISHER
BY: Mitch
ADD ANOTHER CIRCLE BEHIND TO MAKE HIS BODY.
WAH! I LOOK LIKE A BABY!
ROUND
ROUND
NAVEL
WAH!
BIG
First Second
NEW YORK

CAST OF CHARACTERS

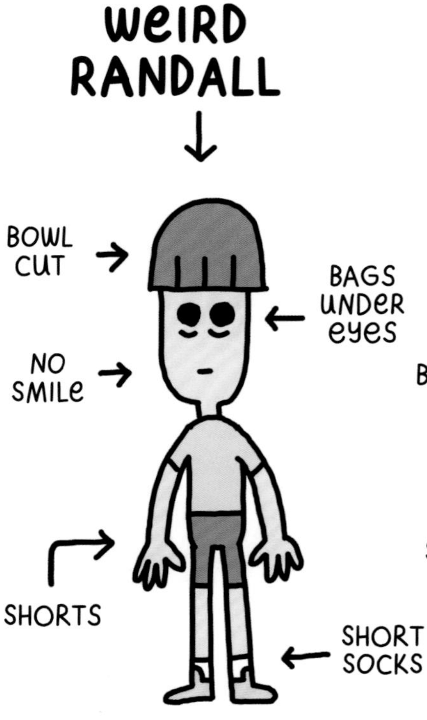

MEGAN

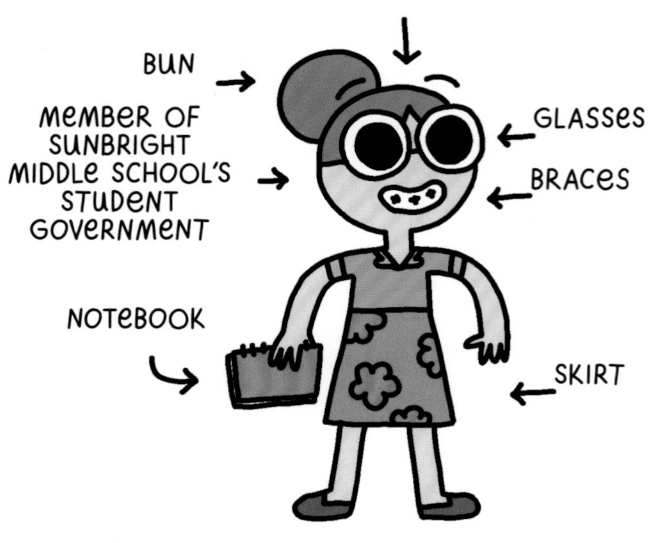

WEIRD RANDALL

BOWL CUT
BAGS UNDER EYES
NO SMILE
SHORTS
SHORT SOCKS

TINA

PONY-TAIL
BOOKS
SWEATER
SKIRT

– HOW TO – READ THIS BOOK

YOUR CHOICES

STILL CONFUSED? READ THIS PAGE AGAIN.	READY TO START? GO TO PAGE 1.

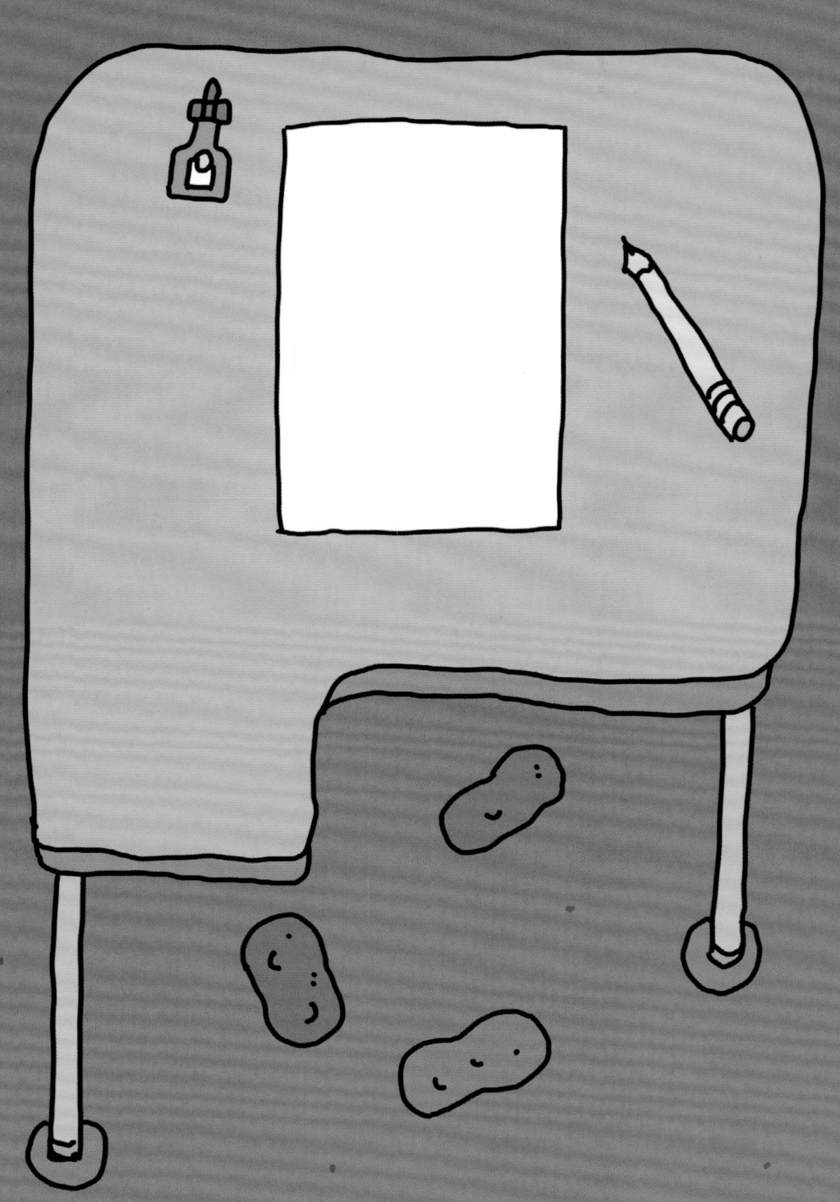

MEGAN'S HERE!

MEGAN!

OLIVIA!

OH HEY!

SO??? DID YOU BRING IT?

ROB?

I LIKE YOUR HAIR!

THANKS! DID I MISS THE BELL?

?

THE DRONE! DID YOU BRING IT?

SHH—YEAH, BUT DON'T TELL ANYONE...

MEGAN! CAN YOU HELP ME WITH SOMETHING?

OH NO!

GO TO CLASS	HELP MR. FISHER
GO TO PAGE 134	GO TO PAGE 37

PHEW! THAT WAS CLOSE!
I'M JUST GLAD MY DRONE IS–

MORE SNEAKS?!
!
!

INTO MY OFFICE, BOTH OF YOU! JOIN THE OTHER SNEAK!
WE'RE SORRY, MR. FISHER!
!

AND I'LL BE TAKING THIS, THANK YOU VERY MUCH!
A NEW TOY! HA HA!
BUT–
!

MY DRONE!
SORRY, ROB.
HEY, GUYS.
THE END

ANYWAY—THERE WAS NO FLYING FISH.
BUMMER.
YEAH.
BUT I THOUGHT IF A FISH WERE FLYING AROUND THE SCHOOL...
...IT WOULD LOVE THE AUDITORIUM!
WHAT FISH WOULDN'T LOVE FLYING AROUND IN SUCH A BIG SPACE?!
I MEAN... I GUESS?
BUT—MELVIN'S NOT HERE, EITHER.
BUT THEN YOU WENT TO THE **LUNCHROOM, RIGHT?** MAYBE THAT'S WHERE MELVIN IS! **LET'S GO!**
HOLD ON— AFTER THE AUDITORIUM...
GO TO PAGE 182

THEY'RE LITTLE BITE MARKS?

VINCENT MUST'VE NIBBLED IT AT HOME! HA HA!

ROB—LOOK!

MINE, TOO! HA HA!

WAIT—WHAT? BUT HOW?!

-SNIFF-
-SNIFF-
GET VINCENT
GO TO PAGE 57
ASK OLIVIA FOR HELP
GO TO PAGE 23

I'M SERIOUS, WEIRD RANDALL! IF YOU'RE GONNA BE IN MY CLASS, YOU ACTUALLY HAVE TO—
OH, GOOD. HERE—
TAKE THESE.
AND THESE.
CLMP!
UM...
...WHY?
WHY WHAT?
WHY ALL THESE POTATOES?!
YOU CAN MAIL THEM TO PEOPLE.
IN THE MAIL.
IT'S LEGAL.
WAIT, YOU'RE GONNA MAIL THESE THINGS?!
IT'S LEGAL.
OH NO!
IT'S MR. FISHER!
RUN
GO TO PAGE 120
KEEP WALKING
GO TO PAGE 145

MEGAN?
JUST A SEC, MISS V. I'M CHECKING ON—

—WEIRD RANDALL?

HEY!

WAIT!

WHERE
HUFF
ARE
HUFF
YOU
HUFF
GOING?

UGH.
THE LUNCH-ROOM?

WEIRD RANDALL—
WHAT ARE YOU DOING?
YOU'RE SUPPOSED TO BE WATCHING FOR THE MACHINE!
GO TO PAGE 5

WHAT?! I'M NOT DOING THAT—NOT IN FRONT OF EVERYONE!
!

GOOD! HA HA HA! I WAS JOKING, ANYWAY—PLUS, I DON'T WANNA SEE YOU DANCE!
HA HA!

SCOTT—THAT IS NOT HOW WE TREAT OUR FRIENDS.
PFT! WHO SAID WE'RE FRIENDS?!

HERE—IT MUST BE FOR SOMETHING IMPORTANT.
NO WAY!
!

THANK YOU, MISS V! I'LL PAY YOU BACK TOMORROW!
BUT—

VINCENT! I'M COMING!

GO TO PAGE 8

GO TO PAGE 144

WAS THAT A DOOR?
CHECK IT OUT WHILE I TAKE A PHOTO!
HOLD STILL...

PIC!

HAH!
GOTCHA!

GUH! YOU SCARED ME, MR. FISHER!
NO ONE SNEAKS AROUND IN MY SCHOOL AND GETS AWAY WITH IT! HAH!

WAIT, WHERE'D IT GO?
AT LEAST I GOT MY PHOTO!
HMPH!

COME WITH ME—
?
PSST!
GO TO PAGE 61

THE SUNBRIGHT MIDDLE SCHOOL NEWSPAPER

MITCH SAVES VENDING MACHINE!

OUR VERY OWN SUNBRIGHT HERO SINGLE-HANDEDLY RAISED MORE THAN ENOUGH FUNDS TO REPLACE THE SNACKS STOLEN FROM THE

READ MITCH'S NOW FAMOUS MR. FISHER COMIC, STARTING ON PAGE 33. BE READY TO LAUGH!

GO TO PAGE 152

WHAT?! THAT'S NOT FAIR—WHAT ABOUT SCOTT?! WE CAN'T JUST LET HIM GET AWAY WITH STEALING SNACKS!!

YOU'RE RIGHT—IT ISN'T FAIR. BUT DON'T WORRY—I'LL LET PRINCIPAL WALTHAM KNOW ONCE THE MEETING'S OVER.

WELL, THANKS FOR YOUR HELP, MEGAN. I'VE GOT TO GET BACK TO MY STUDENTS.

GO TO PAGE 108

ALTHOUGH, MAYBE I CAN TAKE 'IM FOR A RIDE—
!
!
!

—STRAIGHT TO MR. FISHER!
HEY! LET ME OUTTA HERE!!
PIC
PIC
PIC

CHAR—THAT'S IT! THAT'S OUR COVER FOR THE NEWS-PAPER! PRINT IT!
HA HA
HA

SUNBRIGHT NEWSPAPER
MR. H SAVES THE DAY

HA HA HA
HA HA HA
HA HA

CONGRATULATIONS, MR. VILE—LOOKS LIKE YOU MADE THE NEWS.
WHAT? GIMME THAT!
SUNBRIGHT NEWSPAPER
MR. H SAVES THE DAY

PSH—STUPID NEWSPAPER!!
THE END

IN FACT, IT MIGHT NOT BE A BAD IDEA TO TELL EVERYONE MEANINGFUL IN YOUR LIFE THAT YOU LOVE THEM.

IT DOESN'T HAVE TO BE A BIG DEAL, BUT LIFE IS SHORT.

JUST LET THEM KNOW THAT YOU CARE.

>HUG<

HMM. WELL.

NOT JUST **ANYONE** COULD RUN A NEWSPAPER ROUTE—

—OF COURSE, I WAS VERY RESPONSIBLE. A NEWSPAPER ROUTE REQUIRES **DISCIPLINE**...

...SOMETHING YOU KIDS COULD ALWAYS USE MORE OF. HAH!!
CHK
CHK

THERE WE GO! WHAT DO YOU THINK? **MEGAN?**

LIKE I SAID—KIDS THESE DAYS **LACK DISCIPLINE!!**
DIED FROM BOREDOM
THE END

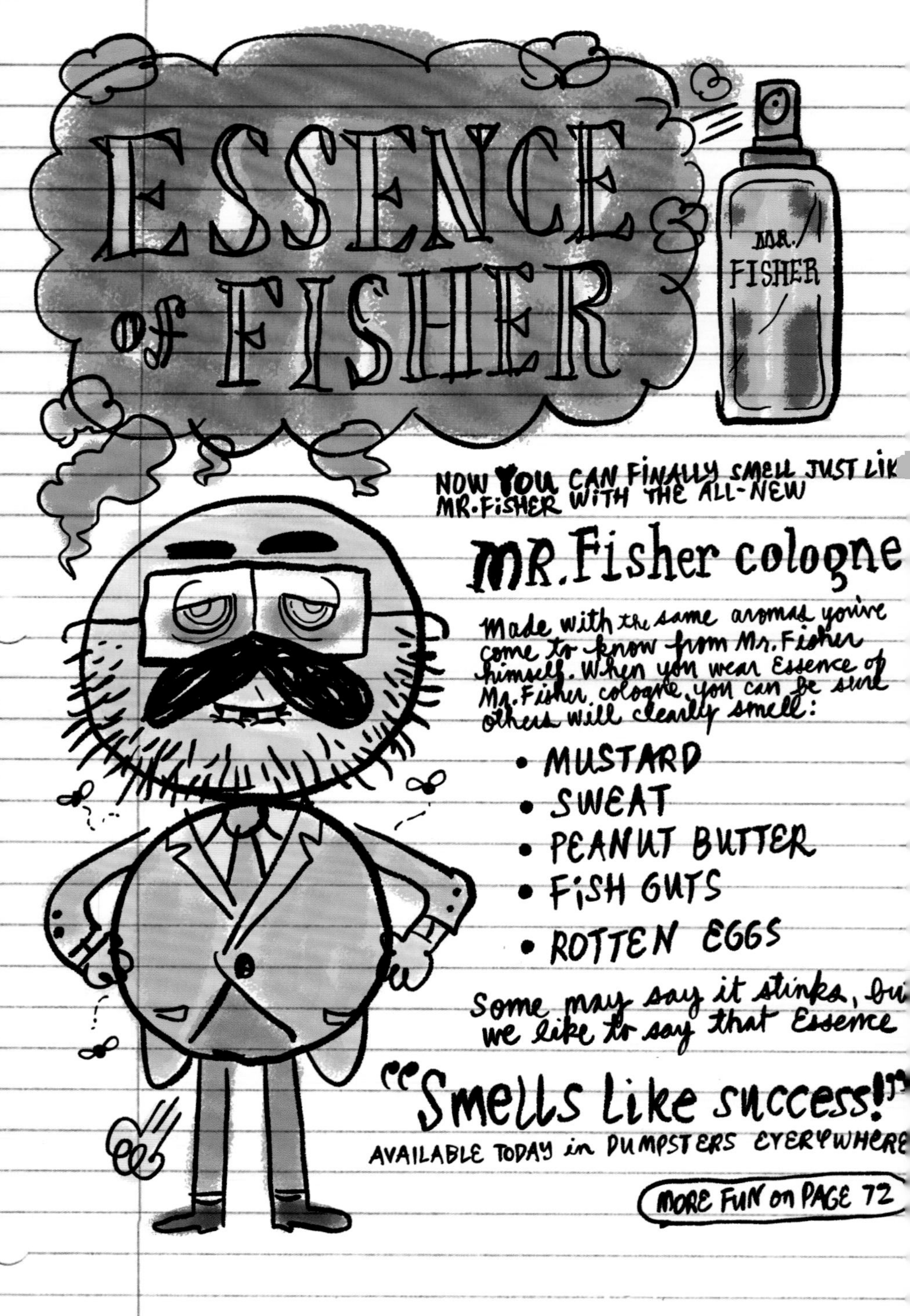
ESSENCE of FISHER
MR. FISHER
NOW YOU CAN FINALLY SMELL JUST LIK
MR. FISHER WITH THE ALL-NEW
MR. Fisher cologne
Made with the same aromas you've come to know from Mr. Fisher himself. When you wear Essence of Mr. Fisher cologne, you can be sure others will clearly smell:
• MUSTARD
• SWEAT
• PEANUT BUTTER
• FISH GUTS
• ROTTEN EGGS
Some may say it stinks, bu
we like to say that Essence
"Smells like success!"
AVAILABLE TODAY in DUMPSTERS EVERYWHERE
MORE FUN on PAGE 72

GO TO PAGE 156

WHOOPS!
!
slip!

CATCH!!

OH!
OH!
OH!

OOF!

OH, THERE YOU ARE! I'VE MISSED YOU. ARE YOU OKAY?
THANKS, WEIRD RANDALL! I WAS—

MELVIN! I'M SO GLAD I FINALLY FOUND YOU!
MELVIN
UM...

OKAY, EVERYONE! HA HA. UM, MEGAN'S BACK WITH MY DRONE AND SOME COPIES. YEAH. SO WE NEED YOUR HELP.
GO TO PAGE 25

THE BABY.
?

HA! BUT IT'S THE SMALLEST OF THEM ALL!
YES—IT'S A LITTLE BIGGER.

WHAT?!

YOU DID IT, WEIRD RANDALL! HA HA! YOU SOLVED THE RIDDLE!
GRRR!
YEAH.
HUFF
HUFF

THAT'S IT—TO MY OFFICE!
BUT YOU SAID—

HOW DARE YOU MAKE ME LOOK LIKE A FOOL IN MY OWN SCHOOL! SHAME ON YOU!
BUT THAT'S NOT FAIR!
FISHER

AND SAY GOODBYE TO YOUR POTATOES—THEY'RE MINE NOW!
ARE YOU GOING TO MAIL THEM?
UGH.
THE END

HMM...I THINK...

...I THINK I'LL WRITE A POEM...

GREAT! LET ME KNOW IF YOU NEED ANY HELP.
MM-HMM...

...HEY, CHAR?
HM?

DO GUYS LIKE POEMS?
HUH? I GUESS. MAYBE. WHY?
TXT
TXT
TXT

YOU THINK DILLON LIKES POETRY?
OH MY, MY! ARE YOU WRITING A POEM FOR DILLON?!

GO TO PAGE 94

BRAAPPPP
BROOOOOOOOOOO
BROMMMM

IT'S SO LOUD!

IT'S SO GOOD!
ROB'S A POET!

THIS DEFINITELY GIVES ME IDEAS FOR LYRICS!!

BUT WAIT—HERE'S THE FINALE!
HEH HEH HEH!
PERFUME SAMPLE
PERFUME
SAMPLE
SAMPLE

INHALE!
GO TO PAGE 60

I SAY WE BUST MITCH OUT FROM FISHER'S OFFICE AND SET OUR FRIEND FREE!

WHO'S WITH ME?!

33

MAYBE YOU DIDN'T HEAR ME...I SAID, **WHO'S WITH ME?!**

HARMONY?
I MEAN... **I WANT TO...**

...BUT I HAVE TO WRITE MY ARTICLE FOR THE PAPER.
YEAH, SAME.
ME TOO.

CAN YOU GIVE ME, LIKE, TEN MINUTES? I'M FINISHING MY ORIGINAL TROM-BONE MUSIC FOR THE SCHOOL PAPER.
GO TO PAGE 195

GO TO PAGE 199

GO TO PAGE 170

ROB'S RIGHT! MITCH PUT HIS LIFE ON THE LINE TO HELP US, SO LET'S NOT LET HIM DOWN!

HERE—EVERYONE TAKE A FEW COPIES. PAY ATTENTION SO YOU CUT AND FOLD IT PROPERLY THE FIRST TIME.
OH NO!

WHAT'S WRONG? ARE YOU OKAY?
I FORGOT TO ASK THE OFFICE FOR KEYS TO THE VENDING MACHINE.

OLIVER!! I MEAN—MR. TWEED HAS THE KEYS. YOU TWO SEEM SO BUSY—I'D BETTER JUST GO AND GET THE KEYS FROM HIM MYSELF. YES. HOW'S MY HAIR?

WHY IS MISS V ACTING SO WEIRD?
AUGH! WHERE'D YOU COME FROM?

...AND THAT'S IT! YOUR PAPERS SHOULD LOOK LIKE THIS WHEN YOU'RE DONE.
GO TO PAGE 147

OH MY GOSH! I JUST REMEMBERED—

—WE'RE STARTING A **NEW UNIT** IN ENGLISH TODAY! I CAN'T MISS IT! **SORRY!**
UNDERSTOOD—**GOOD LUCK!**

SORRY, MR. FISHER! I HOPE YOU'LL UNDERSTAND.
HUFF
WAIT—

WEIRD RANDALL—YOU HAVE TO STAY AND WAIT FOR MR. FISHER'S NEW MACHINE. **OKAY?**
SORRY.

BESIDES—YOU AREN'T EVEN **IN** MY CLASS!
THANKS!

BUT I WANT TO SEE WHAT I'M MISSING OUT ON...
RIGHT, MELVIN?

LATE
BUSTED!
SORRY, MISS V.
GO TO PAGE 122

MR. FISHER!!

TELL ME...
WHO IS YOUR FAVORITE COMPOSER?

UM...M-ME, MR. FISHER?

IT'S A SIMPLE QUESTION, ROBERT.
OH!
RIGHT.
UM...

JUST TELL ME THEIR NAME...
UM.
I WON'T JUDGE YOU.

I'M STILL WAITING, ROBERT.
I KNOW! I KNOW! UM...
GO TO PAGE 90

I WORK WITH TEENS WHO CONSTANTLY DISRESPECT ME.

HOW DO I SHOW THEM THAT I'M IN CHARGE?

HOW DO I GET THEM TO RESPECT ME?

FROM: DISRESPECTED

DEAR DISRESPECTED,
RESPECT GOES BOTH WAYS. SHOW RESPECT TO YOUR TEENS, AND THEY'LL RESPECT YOU BACK.

ALL RIGHT, CLASS—TURN IN YOUR ASSIGNMENTS. I'LL PRINT THE PAPER DURING TODAY'S LUNCH.

-TYPE- -TYPE-

GO TO PAGE 92

WELL, SURE—ERASTUS HAD TO REPEAT HIS EIGHTH-GRADE YEAR.
YOU HELD HIM BACK?!

OH NO—NOT ME. FISHER'S GRANDFATHER—HE WAS PRINCIPAL BACK THEN—SAID YOUNG ERASTUS WASN'T READY FOR NINTH.
WOW—

—YOU HAVE A GOOD MEMORY!
YOU DON'T SOON FORGET SOMEONE LIKE ERASTUS.
HA HA HA

HERE—THIS NEWSPRINT IS FOR YOU. I'M SURE YOU'LL MAKE GOOD USE OF IT.
—OH!

HERE'S THE SCARF I MADE YOU. I HAD FUN ADDING THE DOGS LIKE YOU HAD ASKED.
HUH?

...I DON'T REMEMBER ASKING FOR A SCARF—OR LITTLE DOGS—BUT I LOVE IT! HA HA! THANKS, MRS. BIRMINGHAM!

GO TO PAGE 88

GO TO PAGE 126

OH, HEY, MEGAN—JUST THOUGHT I'D LET YOU KNOW THAT MY **FRIEND**, WHO IS **A PIECE OF OLD GUM**, AND WHO WE'VE SPENT **ALL THIS TIME** LOOKING FOR, HAS BEEN IN MY EAR, RIGHT WHERE I ALWAYS KEEP IT. **HMPH!**

AAAAAAAAAH!!!!!
?
?
?
?
?
?

HMM. FEELS A **LITTLE BETTER**. HOPEFULLY **DILLON'S** STILL INSIDE—
LOCKED

SKRAW!
OH NO. NO, NO, NO—THIS CAN'T BE HAPPENING! WHY WON'T SEAGULLS LEAVE ME ALONE?! OPEN THE DOOR!

SO, UH, YOU THINK **MEGAN'S OKAY?** SHE'S KINDA BEEN **GONE AWHILE**...
MELVIN WANTS TO SHOW YOU A TRICK. READY?

HELP!
THE END

Yes, Dillon?
MEGAN. YOUR TIME IS UP.
HUH?

Dillon
XOXO
M + D
TRUE LOVE
MEGAN
DILLON
M+D
Dillon
Megan Pepper

EVERYONE'S CONTRIBUTIONS WILL BE ADDED TO THE PAPER, WHICH WILL BE PRINTED AND DISTRIBUTED TO THE ENTIRE SCHOOL WITHIN THE NEXT HOUR.
!!

WAIT—MISS V! THAT'S THE WRONG PAPER! PLEASE DON'T PRINT IT! I—
HEY, MEGAN...

...IT'S PRETTY COOL THAT YOU FINISHED YOUR ARTICLE SO QUICKLY!
MY LIFE IS OVER!!
HEH HEH
THE END

① DRAW A BIG OL' GIANT CIRCLE FOR MR. FISHER'S NOGGIN.
i'm so smort.
BIG
WARNING
YOU'LL NEED AT LEAST 5 PIECES OF PAPER TO DRAW HIS GIANT HEAD
HOW TO DRAW MR. FISHER
BY: mitch
② ADD ANOTHER CIRCLE BELOW TO MAKE HIS BODY.
WAH! I LOOK LIKE A BABY!
ROUND
ROUND
NAVEL
③ ADD BEARD CONTENTS AND ADD STINK LINES (USE GENEROUSLY!)
WAH!
MORE ON PAGE 176

MRNF MRR HRMF!

—MITCH?
SHH—I'M TRACKING THE SUNBRIGHT MUCK MAN FOR THE SCHOOL NEWSPAPER. ALSO...

...I DREW THIS.
WAH!

HEE HEE! IS THAT MR. FISHER?
SHH!

SO...DO WE JUST SIT AND WAIT?

GO TO PAGE 159

GO TO PAGE 219

GO TO PAGE 167

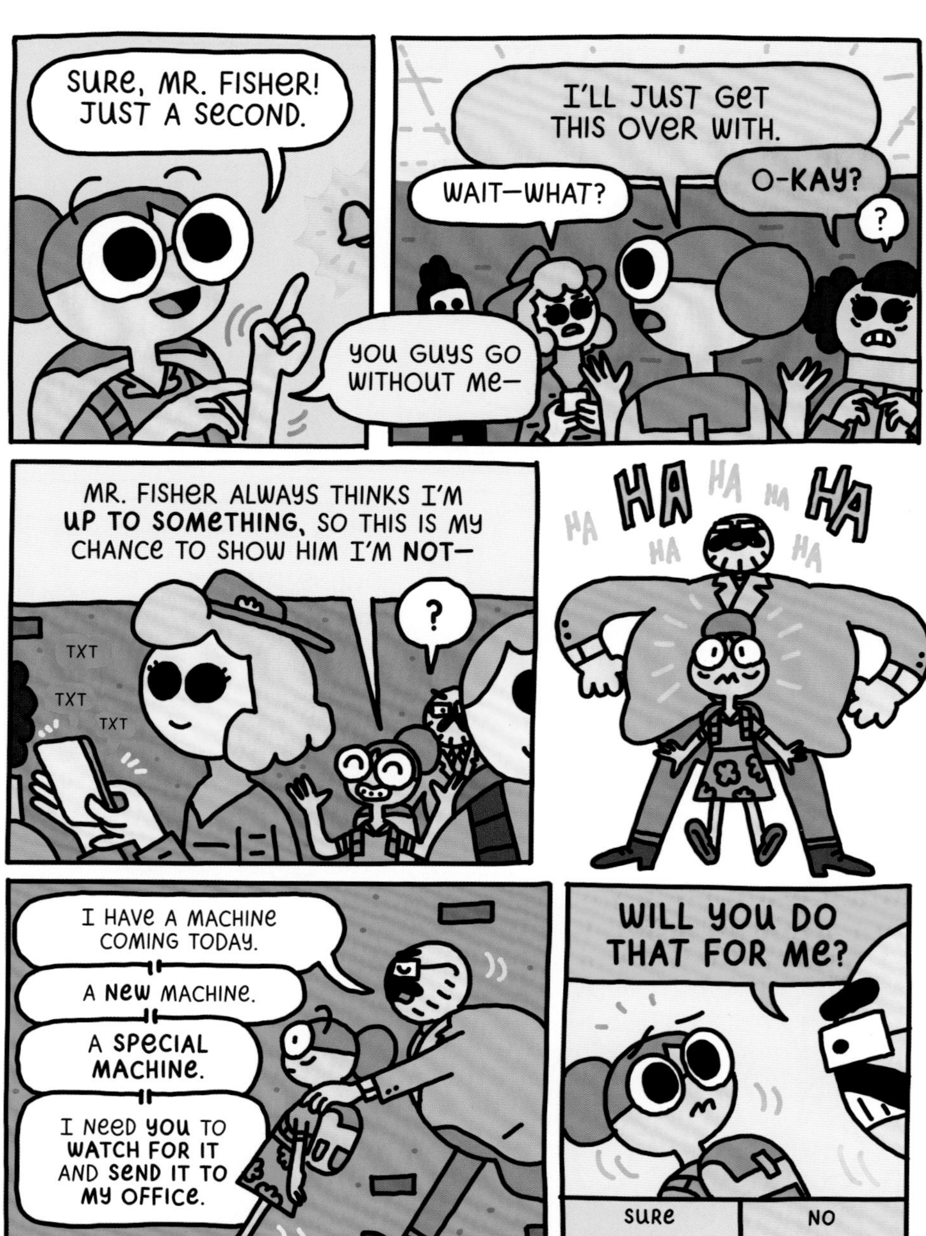

SURE	NO
GO TO PAGE 68	GO TO PAGE 153

FAVE MOVIE?
THERE—
I JUST FINISHED WRITING MY ESSAY BY HAND. I FORMATTED THE DOCUMENT FOR THE FRONT PAGE OF THE CLASS NEWSPAPER!
EX-CUSE ME?
SORRY TO INTERRUPT.
UM—I HAVE A PIZZA ORDER HERE.
...FOR TODD?
TYLER JUST MESSAGED BACK. HIS FAVORITE MOVIE IS...SPACE GOBLINS?
YOU TODD?
FINALLY! I'M SO HUNGRY!
SPACE GOBLINS IS LEGITERALLY THE BEST MOVIE!!
—OOPS.
MY ESSAY!
MY PIZZA!
GO TO PAGE 93

GO TO PAGe 128

SHOWERS ARE CLEAR.

FIRST SET OF LOCKERS IS CLEAR.

MITCH—LOOK!

I'VE BEEN WAIT-ING FOR THIS MO-MENT ALL MY LIFE...
GO TO PAGE 154

GO TO PAGE 175

GO TO PAGE 155

GO TO PAGE 224

ALL RIGHT—I'VE GOTTA SEE WHAT PEOPLE ARE SENDING YOU!
STICK
I'LL START OPENING—YOU JUST KEEP DOING...WHATEVER YOU'RE DOING.
FROM "FRAGRANCE & BOUQUET"?
FRAGRANCE & BOUQUET
Weird Randall
c/o Sunbright
Middle School
Attn: Ms. Valentine
WHAT EVEN IS THAT?
PHEW! WHATEVER'S INSIDE HAS A VERY STRONG SMELL!
COUGH! COUGH!
PERFUME SAMPLES?!
DID YOU ORDER THESE, WEIRD RANDALL?
WHAT ELSE IS IN HERE?
DOG TREATS
COUPONS
FREE!
INVISIBLE INK
OOH—I'LL TRADE YOU A SODA FOR THAT INVISIBLE INK?
I DID IT! I THINK THE COPY MACHINE'S READY!!
HERE—COPY THIS.
PHEW!
I'LL ALSO ADD WHAT I MADE FOR THE PAPER!
?
SO? YOU WANNA TRADE ME?
SURE
GO TO PAGE 86
NAH
GO TO PAGE 185

VINCENT!
DON'T WORRY—
MR. H WILL GET
YOU OUT QUICK!
F33

JUST **STAY HERE** WHILE
I—WAIT. I **KNOW** YOU'LL
STAY HERE, BUT JUST...
I'LL BE
RIGHT
BACK!
F33

OH, GOOD—MR. H!
?

MY PET HEDGEHOG
IS SUPER CUTE AND
SUPER STUCK IN
THE VENDING MACHINE!
CAN YOU UNLOCK IT?
I'M SORRY,
MEGAN, BUT
MR. TWEED
HAS MY KEYS—

LET'S GO!
HIS CLASS IS
OVER HERE!

OLIVER! I NEED
THOSE **KEYS** REAL
QUICK—I'LL BRING
'EM **RIGHT BACK**.
AH!

THANKS, MR. TW—

SNATCH!

GO TO PAGE 99

...RIGHT THERE. YES—THAT'LL DO. GOOD DAY!
ENJOY!
OKAY, MR. FISHER—NOW CAN I GO? I'M LATE FOR CLASS.
NO, NO, NO...
...WE HAVEN'T FINISHED TALKING ABOUT NEWSPAPERS!
THERE'S MORE TO SAY?
HERE—OPEN THE TOP.
IS THIS NECESSARY?
THIS
RUNNING A PAPER ROUTE WAS IMPORTANT BUSINESS—I'D WAKE UP BEFORE DAWN, ROLL PAPERS...
...FIT THE RUBBER BANDS, THEN TAKE TO MY BICYCLE!!
GO TO PAGE 15

I'LL NEED THOSE STAMPS.
WE'LL NEED SOME **FUEL!**
WAIT—
THIS IS SO **DUMB.**

YES—**ONE LARGE MUSHROOM,** PLEASE...SUNBRIGHT MIDDLE.
I CAN PROBABLY FIND A NEWSPAPER TEMPLATE ON MY **TABLET.**

UM.
?

WAIT—
WEIRD RANDALL ACTUALLY LEFT?

CAN I DO A **MUSIC COLUMN?**
AND CAN I DO A **DANCE AND TRAVEL SECTION?**
STOP WEIRD RANDALL
GO TO PAGE 6
IGNORE WEIRD RANDALL
GO TO PAGE 193

THE MANY FACES OF MR. FISHER

BY YOUR PA MITCH

HAPPY

JOYFUL

STINKY

SAD

TIRED

HUNGRY

SMORT

REMEMBERING

KISSING

LEARN TO DRAW ON PAGE 33

...I THINK I'M GONNA—
!

EVERYONE OUT—NOW!!
WAIT—WHAT?
WHY?
DON'T TELL ME WHAT TO DO!

YARK!

OH. MY. GASP.
DID SHE JUST—
—EW! DON'T SAY IT!
OOF—
THAT SMELL!

THE GOOD NEWS IS...

...I FEEL MUCH BETTER.
OH, GOOD!
PHEW!
WHAT THE H*CK, LILY? STOP LOOKING AT ME THAT WAY!
SNIFF

...THE BAD NEWS IS...
GO TO PAGE 168

GO TO PAGE 188

COME ON, MEGAN—
YOU CAN COME UP
WITH SOMETHING.
THINK! TEN MINUTES
IS ENOUGH TIME. PLUS...
...JUST THINK OF HOW
IMPRESSED DILLON WILL BE
WHEN YOU PULL THIS OFF!
Oh, Megan?
Yes, sweet Dillon?
I really like
what you did for
the newspaper...
and I really
like you, too!
Oh, Dillon!
MEGAN?
GO TO
PAGE 32

BACK HERE—WE'LL HAVE TO DUCK PAST THE MAIN OFFICE!

THERE IT IS—
?
—MY DRONE!!

ROB—WAIT!

GO TO PAGE 2

GO TO PAGE 118

GO TO PAGE 100

ASSEMBLE THE COPY MACHINE
GO TO PAGE 169

ASK FOR HELP IN ASSEMBLING
GO TO PAGE 109

!

MR. H? WHERE ARE YOU GOING? WHAT ABOUT THE GARBAGE?
FOLLOW ME!

OLIVER! ER, MR. TWEED...SORRY TO INTERRUPT—DO YOU STILL HAVE THE VEND-ING MACHINE KEYS?
AH!

CATCH!
THANKS!
NOW—WHICH WAY TO YOUR CLASS?
OVER HERE!

QUICK—I NEED ALL YOUR TOYS, UNWANTED FOOD, BOOKS, CLOTHING ITEMS...ANYTHING AND EVERYTHING YOU HAVE BUT DON'T NEED OR WANT!!

?

GO TO PAGE 63

GO TO PAGE 215

MR. FISHER'S VACATION PART ONE

A "MR. FISHER COMIC STORY" BY MITCH

READ MORE ON PAGE 194

YES—IT'S OBVIOUS YOU'VE BEEN CRYING.
WAIT— WHAT?
SNIFF

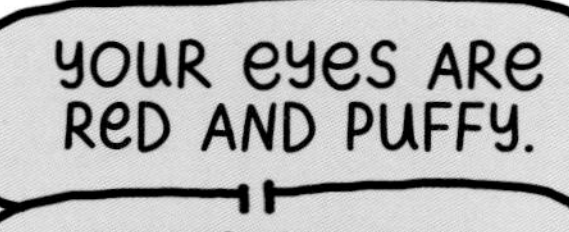
YOUR EYES ARE RED AND PUFFY.
YOUR HAIR IS FRAZZLED.
YOU'RE STILL SNIFFLING.
YOUR MASCARA IS SMEARED AND RUNNY.

I **KNEW** IT! I'M A **MESS**!
IT'S TRUE.
SNRK!
OH!
MY!
OPEN

BACK TO YOUR SEAT, RANDALL.
I DON'T HAVE A SEAT.

SORRY ABOUT THAT, CLASS.
NOW—**WHERE** WERE WE?
Newspap
CLOSE!

DO WE STILL GOTTA MAKE THE DUMB FREAKIN' NEWSPAPER?

GO TO PAGE 73

SO, THERE'S MY SONG!
WELL...
CLAP
CLAP
CLAP
COUGH!
COUGH!

...WHAT DO YOU THINK?

OH, MAN— IT'S GREAT.
YEAH! I LOVE IT!

I REEK OF FLOWERS AND SWEETNESS!
HOW DO I GET THIS OFF?!
UGH!
COUGH!
COUGH!

BUT, SCOTT—I THINK YOU SMELL SO GOOD!
WHAT? STOP IT. GET AWAY FROM ME!

OOG—TOO, TOO MUCH PERFUME...

GO TO PAGE 49

GO TO PAGE 117

HI. I HAVE A GIRLFRIEND AND I PLAY THE BASS.

MY GIRLFRIEND IS SUPER FREAKING HOT BUT SHE LIKES HUGGING ME AT SCHOOL BUT I DON'T LIKE IT.

WHAT DO I DO?

-HEARTBROKEN

GO TO PAGE 187

DANCE
GO TO PAGE 137

DON'T DANCE
GO TO PAGE 7

GO TO PAGE 218

GO TO PAGE 211

HOOMF!

GOTCHA!

WHY'D YOU RUN
FROM ME, VINCENT?
I WOULDN'T LET—

—OH NO. I KNOW
THIS ROOM...

HA! SO THIS EXPLAINS THE
LITTLE DROPPINGS ALL AROUND
THE SCHOOL—LET'S CALL YOUR
PARENTS AND EXPLAIN IT TO THEM!
UGH...YES,
MR. FISHER.

SNIFF SNIFF
DO YOU
SMELL GRANOLA?
THE
END

SURE! YEAH, I CAN DO THAT.
HMM.

SO I JUST WAIT HERE 'TIL IT COMES?

WHY ARE YOU SO WEIRD?

AND SO THE WAITING BEGINS...
-SIGH-

-SIGH-
WHAT ARE WE WAITING FOR?
WEIRD RANDALL!

THIS IS FUN.
I LIKE WAITING.
!
MEGAN!

MEGAN! HEY—DO YOU MIND HELPING ME WITH SOMETHING REAL QUICK?
HI, MR. H!
I'M WAITING.
HELP
GO TO PAGE 115
GO TO CLASS
GO TO PAGE 26

OKAY, YOU GOT SOME-THING FROM THE MACHINE. **THEN WHAT?**

OH—I DIDN'T HAVE ANY MONEY, SO I WENT TO THE OFFICE TO ASK PRINCIPAL WALTHAM FOR A DOLLAR...
UGH...

...BUT MRS. GLADSTONE SAID HE'S IN A MEETING.
IT'S TRUE. HI, MEGAN!

SO, I TOOK OFF MY SHOES—
WAIT—
WHAT?!

—TO SEE HOW FAR I COULD SLIDE DOWN THE HALL IN MY SOCKS.
SHHH
HHHGH
HW

I AM SO VERY **BORED** RIGHT NOW.
I SLID RIGHT INTO—
GO TO PAGE 131

SORRY, RANDALL— ER, UM, I MEAN, WEIRD RANDALL...
...THAT FEELS SO MEAN TO SAY!

NO POTATOES. YOU AREN'T EVEN IN MY CLASS!
SAD.

WAIT—I HAVE AN IDEA! DOES ANYONE HAVE MONEY?
PSH! I ALWAYS HAVE CASH—MY DAD'S SUPER RICH.

SCOTT—COPY YOUR MONEY! PUT IT ON THE MACHINE—YOU'LL MAKE US ALL RICH!
YES!
DILLON, YOU'RE A GENIUS!

SCOTT!
SCOTT!
SCOTT!
SCOTT!
WHAT THE JUNK?

LOUDER! HA HA! LOUDER!!
UGH.
SHEESH.

SCOTT!
SCOTT!
SCOTT!
SCOTT!
HA HA
HA HA
HA

GO TO PAGE 30

OUTTA MY WAY!
HEY!
UR DUM

I'M SPENDING ALL MY MONEY AND BUYING ALL YOUR JUNK, SO NO ONE ELSE GETS ANY!!
NOT COOL, SCOTT!
$50
$50
$50

HA HA! LOSERS!
WHY'S HE HAVE TO BE SO MEAN?!

AT LEAST WE PROBABLY MADE ENOUGH MONEY TO RESTOCK THE VENDING MACHINE.
HEY, LOOK—THERE'S SOMETHING LEFT!!

25¢
25¢

WHAT IS IT?
?

MELVIN!
I DO NOT UNDERSTAND YOU.
KISS KISS
THE END

CONTINUED ON PAGE 214

THE PAPER! OF COURSE! YES—LET'S GET STARTED!!

SO WE JUST FIND NEWS TO PUT IN?

THAT'S RIGHT!
WELL... KIND OF.

DOES IT HAVE TO BE NEWS?
CAN WE DO STUFF WE LIKE?

LIKE—NOT NEWS?
OR AT LEAST NEWS ABOUT STUFF WE LIKE?

YEAH!
LIKE THE NEW UPDATE FOR WREKKER?

GO TO PAGE 78

GO TO PAGE 192

Mr. Fisher's Big Day

Part 2/2

A Lil Comic Story by Mitch

MORE INFORMATION ON PAGE 48

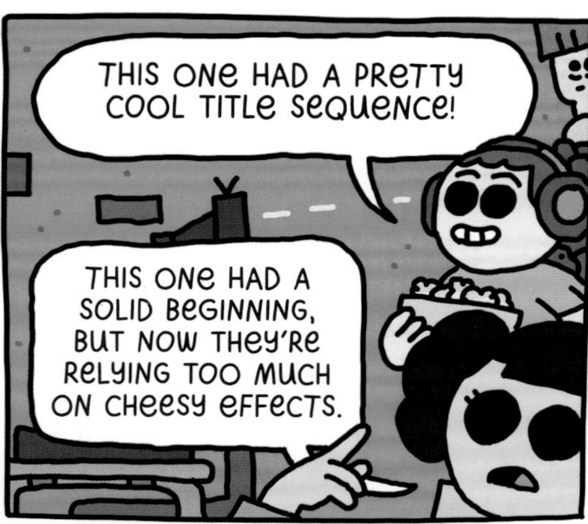

GO TO PAGE 227

...IT SEEMS MY NEW MACHINE HAS ARRIVED!!

GREAT!
COPY
PRINTER

SO I CAN GO NOW?
Erastus R. Fisher
(SIGN HERE)

NO—I NEED YOUR HELP.
THIS WAY!

BUT YOUR MACHINE'S HERE—I THOUGHT THAT'S WHAT YOU WANTED.

KEEP IT COMING...

GO TO PAGE 46

YES! OF COURSE!
THIS IS YOUR PAPER—
IT IS?
IT CAN BE WHATEVER YOU WANT IT TO BE!

COOL! CAN I MAKE DRAWINGS?

OR WRITE ABOUT MOVIES I LIKE?

CAN I WRITE MY OWN ESSAY?

YES—THESE ARE ALL GREAT IDEAS!

CAN YOU GET ME A WHOLE BUNCH OF POSTAGE STAMPS?

RANDALL—DON'T YOU HAVE YOUR OWN CLASS TO ATTEND?

GO TO PAGE 47

OKAY, EVERYONE STAY CALM. DON'T PANIC. REMEMBER YOUR TRAINING.
WHAT TRAINING?

GASP! THE DOOR!

HUFF HUFF HUFF HUFF
CLOSE
LOCK

THE OFFICE!

MRS. GLADSTONE? I AM NOT HERE– AND DON'T LET HIM IN!!
WHO IS THIS?

FISH-MAN! YOU IN THERE?
YIPE!!

WHATDOWEDO? WHEREDOWEGO? NONONONONO!
HEY!

OPEN UP, FISH-MAN!

GO TO PAGE 50

CLICK!
CREEEEAK

GASP!
CLINK

MEGAN!
ARE YOU OKAY?
UGH.

THANKS >HUFF< FOR HIDING ME >HUFF<, BUT CAN WE PROMISE TO NEVER >HUFF< DO THAT AGAIN?!

HERE—HA HA! THAT WAS AWESOME!
UGHH... THANKS?

OH!
JUST
ONE
MORE
THING...
GO TO PAGE 27

GO TO PAGE 210

WELL, THERE'S NO ROOM IN THE SCHOOL BUDGET TO BUY NEW SNACKS.

DON'T WE HAVE, LIKE, A FUNDRAISER?

WE USE MONEY FROM SELLING SNACKS TO BUY NEW ONES. SINCE WE CAN'T SELL THESE, WE CAN'T BUY NEW SNACKS. NO MORE VENDING MACHINES. NO MORE SNACKS.

GO BACK TO CLASS GO TO PAGE 141

TELL MR. FISHER GO TO PAGE 165

ROB TOLD YOU THE NAME. NOW YOU'RE JUST ACTING LIKE A BULLY!

THERE YOU ARE!

SO YOU DIDN'T HAVE TIME TO HELP ME— BUT YOU HAD TIME TO HIDE? HUH?!
OOPS!

ALL OF YOU GO TO CLASS—
—EXCEPT FOR YOU TWO!

AND...
LIKE THAT, MR. FISHER?
GOOD—NOW TOGETHER.
FISHER

BROOOONK!
HAWMP!
UGH!
THE END

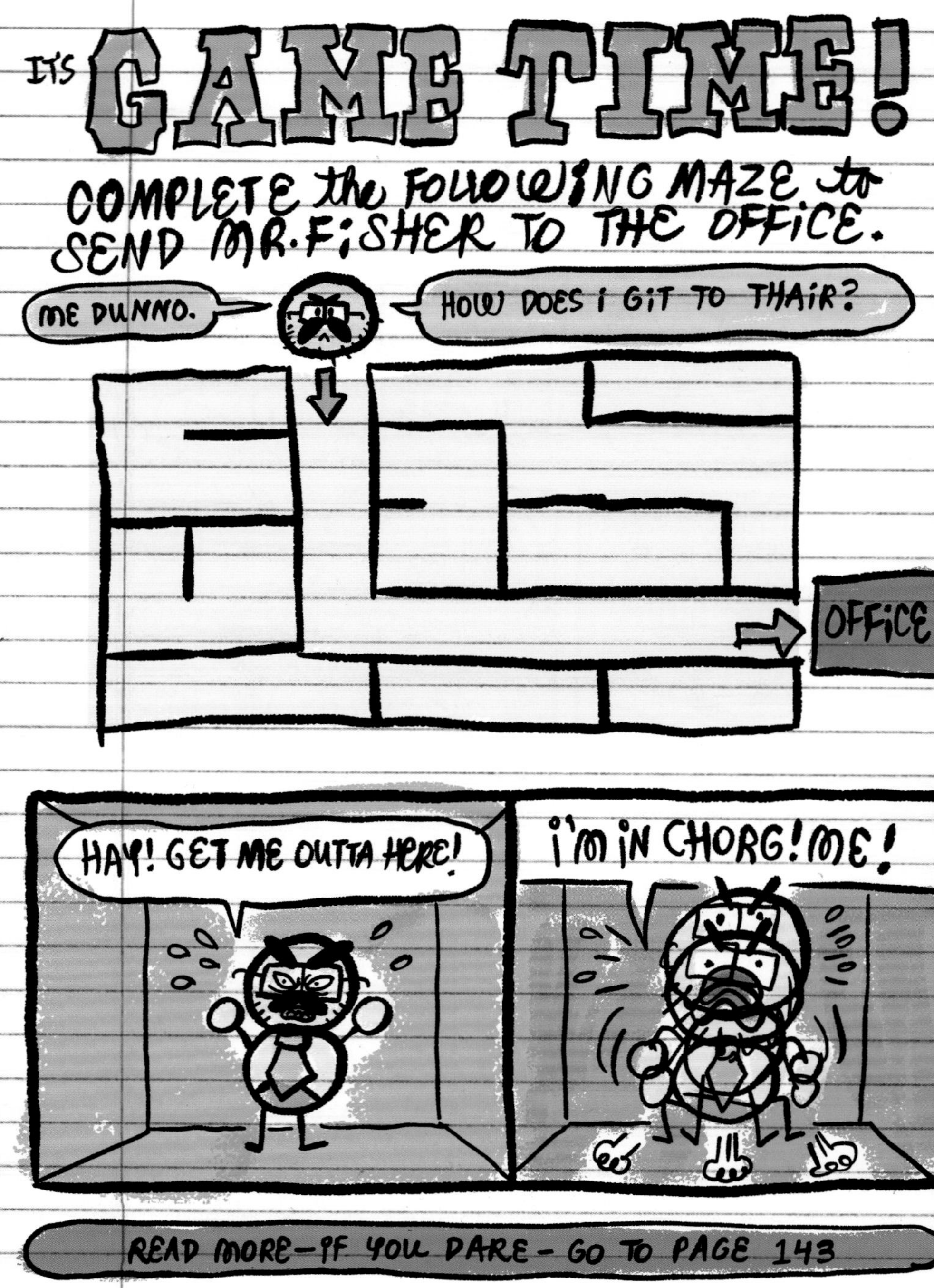
IT'S GAME TIME!
COMPLETE the FOLLOWING MAZE to SEND MR. FISHER TO THE OFFICE.
ME DUNNO.
HOW DOES I GIT TO THAIR?
OFFICE
HAY! GET ME OUTTA HERE!
I'M IN CHORG! ME!
READ MORE—IF YOU DARE—GO TO PAGE 143

GO TO PAGE 161

SURE! THIS SAMPLE BOTTLE OF INVISIBLE INK FOR YOUR SODA.
THANK YOU!

WHOA—THAT'S AWESOME! IT'S LIKE IT DISAPPEARS!

OKAY, CLASS, IT SEEMS THAT ROB HAS PUT TOGETHER THIS COPY MACHINE AND IT RUNS WELL!
THANK YOU, ROB!
THANK YOU, ROB!
HA HA! OKAY!

WE'RE SO CLOSE TO BEING ABLE TO PRINT OUR CLASS PAPER!
ALL WE NEED NOW IS A COVER STORY...

...ANY IDEAS? TINA?
HUH? UGH... TOO TIRED... NEED FUEL...
WAIT—

—I HAVE AN IDEA!
I'M JUST GONNA BORROW THIS FOR A SEC—'K, CHAR?
HA! GO FOR IT!
GO TO PAGE 217

YOU'RE RIGHT—THAT **WOULD** BE FUN...BUT WE'RE NOT **ALLOWED** TO SELL THE PAPER—**IT HAS TO BE FREE**.

IS THAT ALL YOU WANTED TO ASK ME?

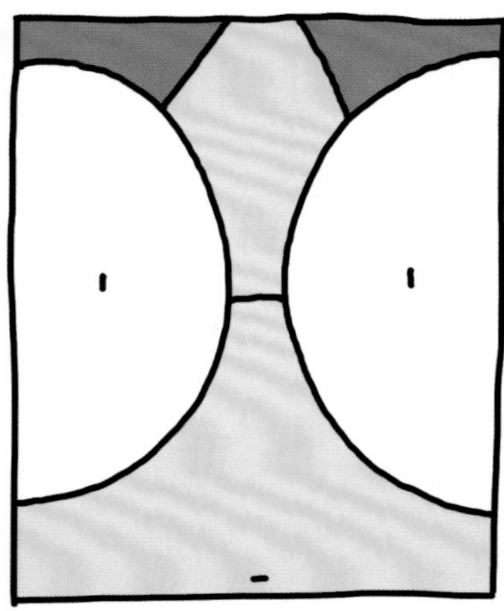

GO TO PAGE 173

REPORT ON THE SCHOOL TALENT SHOW GO TO PAGE 103
WRITE A POEM GO TO PAGE 20
ARTICLE ON ART DISPLAY GO TO PAGE 208

DEFEND ROB
GO TO PAGE 83

RUN AWAY
GO TO PAGE 197

DID I JUST HEAR SOMETHING **SNAP?!**
SCOTT DID IT! HE BROKE THE MACHINE!

IT'S ROB'S FAULT! HE FREAKING DISTRACTED ME!!

OKAY, OKAY, EVERYONE JUST CALM DOWN.
SCOTT—I NEED YOU TO GO TO THE OFFICE **NOW**.
I DON'T HAVE TO! YOU CAN'T MAKE ME. NO ONE CAN!
EVERYTHING GOING OKAY?

MR. H—SCOTT BROKE THE COPY MACHINE, AND HE WON'T GO TO THE OFFICE LIKE MISS V TOLD HIM!
?
SO?!

WELL, HE'S NOT GOING **ANYWHERE** NOW!!
!

GO TO PAGE 13

I WANT EVERY-ONE'S ATTENTION!!

WHO DID THIS? WHO WROTE THE SO-CALLED ADVICE COLUMN IN MISS V'S CLASS PAPER?!

UH-OH!
YIKES!

WHAT DID YOU WRITE?
NOTHING BAD—I DON'T KNOW WHY HE'S UPSET.

LOOK—MR. FISHER'S SO MAD, HE'S HAVING TROUBLE TALKING!
RAM-GREM-GRRMR-ROGGUM-CRAW-SKRF

NO ONE LEAVES UNTIL I FIND OUT WHO WROTE THIS—GOT IT?!
CONFESS
GO TO PAGE 157
STAY SILENT
GO TO PAGE 226

GO TO PAGE 130

GO TO PAGE 228

GO TO PAGE 119

GO TO PAGE 149

FINALLY—I'M STARVING!
YOU'RE TODD?
CHECK IT OUT!
WAIT— MITCH DREW YOU?!
IT'S SO GOOD!

HOLD IT!
WAIT.
HEY!
YOINK!
YOU OWE ME—

—ELEVEN BUCKS.
OH.
UMM...

HEY, SO, ANYONE HAVE SOME MONEY I CAN BORROW?
WHAT?
HEY!
—OVER HERE!
KIK

IT'S BEEN A WHILE...
BOOMP!
BUT...
...I USED TO PLAY!
DRIBBLE DRIBBLE DRIBBLE

GO TO PAGE 66

AH, YES—THIS IS MUCH BETTER.
IT IS?
?

ACTUALLY, THIS IS RATHER QUITE GOOD!
UGH.
HA

IN HERE.
SIT.

THERE.

READ THIS UNTIL SCHOOL LETS OUT—MAYBE YOU'LL LEARN SOMETHING ABOUT RESPECT!
!
RESPECT
THE END

MR. FISHER!

FOLLOW ME—ALL OF YOU. I WILL OPEN THE MACHINE.
BUT—

WELL, WELL, WELL... WHAT IS THIS?
UNLOCK

NOW WHAT'S A HEDGEPIG DOING IN MY VENDING MACHINE?
HMM... I SEEM TO REMEMBER A RULE AGAINST BRINGING PETS TO SCHOOL.
LOCK!

WE'RE SORRY! IT WON'T HAPPEN AGAIN!
ALL OF YOU— TO MY OFFICE!!
!!

SO.
I DON'T WANT TO HEAR A PEEP OUT OF ANYONE. GOT IT?!
YES, MR. FISHER.
!!
NAUGHTY
THE END

SPECIAL COLLECTIONS, MRS. BIRMINGHAM? LIKE SPECIAL BOOKS?

SPECIAL COLLECTIONS...
SPECIAL
COLLECTIONS
UNLOCK!

...SOME OF THESE ARE FILED AS REFERENCE BOOKS—THEY CAN'T BE CHECKED OUT!
REALLY?

SEE THESE? THESE ARE THE PERSONAL JOURNALS OF SUNBRIGHT'S VERY FIRST PRINCIPAL FISHER.
WAIT—LIKE MR. FISHER?!

MR. FISHER'S GRANDFATHER WAS OUR FIRST PRINCIPAL. MR. FISHER'S FATHER WAS OUR SECOND PRINCIPAL.
SO THAT'S WHY MR. FISHER ALWAYS WANTS TO BE IN CHARGE!
HA HA
GO TO PAGE 163

GO TO PAGE 198

OKAY.
...CHARGER...
...GOT IT!

WHOA—
THAT'S A LONG CORD!
WE HAVE POWER!
-PLUG!-

YES! IT'S WORKING!
I GOT A TEXT!
ALL RIGHT! Y'ALL READY FOR THIS?!
—WHOOPS!
TRIP!

HUH?
YOINK!
CLIK!
15
CLONK!

OH NO!!
GO TO PAGE 24

THEY ALL SOUND PRETTY FUN, BUT...

...I DEFINITELY HAVE SOME THINGS TO SAY ABOUT THE SCHOOL TALENT SHOW! HA HA!

OKAY—GREAT! IT'S ALL YOURS.
YES!

WE HAVE ABOUT TWENTY-FIVE MINUTES LEFT IN CLASS TO FINISH—LET ME KNOW IF YOU HAVE ANY QUESTIONS OR NEED HELP.
SURE, MISS V—THANKS!

I COULD WRITE A WHOLE BOOK ON THE TALENT SHOW! LET'S SEE...

HEY—WHAT HAPPENED TO MY NOTEBOOK?!
GO TO PAGE 4

I DON'T AGREE WITH EVERYTHING SCOTT SAID, BUT...

...LET'S DO IT—
LET'S FREE MITCH!
THIS IS A BAD IDEA. EVERYONE PLEASE TAKE YOUR SEATS.

LOOKS LIKE IT'S JUST US.
BEING MAD MAKES ME HUNGRY! HEY—GIMME FIVE BUCKS.

WHAT? SORRY, BUT I DON'T HAVE ANY MONEY.
WELL, MINE'S IN MY BACKPACK—IN CLASS.
ANYWAY...

WHOA—WHAT ARE YOU DOING? YOU'RE NOT SUPPOSED TO SHAKE—
I DON'T CARE ABOUT RULES!
CNK!
CRNK!
KNK!

HA HA HA HA HA
EMPTY
?

GO TO PAGE 82

GO TO PAGE 178

OKAY—YOU KNOW WHAT? I'M SORRY, WEIRD RANDALL, BUT I JUST CAN'T TAKE ANY MORE OF THIS!

I'M SURE YOU HAD A GRAND ADVENTURE AND EVERYTHING— BUT I'M GOING BACK TO CLASS!
GOOD LUCK FINDING MELVIN!

HOW AM I GOING TO EXPLAIN THIS TO MISS V?

?

THESE ALMOST LOOK LIKE—

!!
GO TO PAGE 34

GO TO PAGE 202

SO WHAT ARE WE GONNA SNACK ON DURING BORING CLASSES AND BEFORE AND AFTER LUNCH AND DURING READING TIME? IT'S NOT FAIR!

ANYONE ELSE WANNA HELP?
ME TOO!
AND ME!
OOH—ME!
CAN I HELP—
TRIP!
WHOA!
CRASH!
—OOF!!
OOPS.
HA HA HA HA HA HA
OLIVIA! ARE YOU OKAY?
GO TO PAGE 81

WAIT—A **WHAT?**
A SCHOOL SONG—
THOUGH YOU'LL NEED **LYRICS** TO GO WITH THE MUSIC.
?
THAT SOUNDS **FUN!** HA HA!
WE CAN MAKE IT A **CONTEST!**

I'LL GIVE A WHOLE TWELVE-PACK OF SODA TO THE WINNER.
!
COOL! I'LL WORK WITH MISS V ON THE RULES TO PUT IN THE PAPER.

HOLD UP, MITCH—**NOW** I WANT **SODA!**
ME TOO!
HA HA HA HA HA HA HA HA

HEY—**ANYONE** CAN ENTER THE CONTEST, **RIGHT?** NOT JUST ROB AND HARMONY?
I THINK SO. THAT'S WHAT MISS V SAID.
HMM...

...LET'S DO IT! LET'S COME UP WITH OUR OWN SCHOOL SONG LYRICS! YOU IN?
GO TO PAGE 206

WAIT A SECOND—ROB! DO YOU STILL HAVE YOUR DRONE?
IT'S PUT AWAY, MISS V! IT'S BEEN IN MY BACKPACK THE WHOLE TIME!

RELAX—YOU AREN'T IN ANY TROUBLE. YOU MIGHT ACTUALLY BE ABLE TO SAVE US, ROB—US AND MITCH.
WRITE WRITE
WRITE WRITE

ROB—CAN YOU FLY THIS NOTE TO MITCH IN MR. FISHER'S OFFICE?
I'VE NEVER FLOWN IT INSIDE BEFORE.

YOU CAN DO THIS, ROB—WE'RE ALL COUNTING ON YOU. DO IT—DO IT FOR MITCH.
WELL, OKAY. I'LL TRY FOR MITCH.
ATTACH

HUMMM MMMMM

OKAY—WE'RE IN THE AIR!

GO TO PAGE 65

GO TO PAGE 204

GO TO PAGE 158

UM—I CAN, MISS V.
!
NO—
ME!

OH! MEGAN AND TINA?
WELL
UM
I WASN'T EXPECTING THIS.

I SUPPOSE YOU CAN WORK TOGETHER!
JOINT EDITORS IN CHIEF!
YOU'RE SUPPOSED TO BE OUT HERE WATCHING FOR MY MACHINE!
HEY!

WAIT—DID YOU SAY EDITOR IN CHIEF?
ARE YOU MAKING A NEWSPAPER?

I WAS ASSISTANT EDITOR WHEN I WAS YOUR AGE...
...I SHOULD'VE BEEN CHIEF!
GO TO PAGE 179

OF COURSE, MR. H!
WEIRD RANDALL—CAN YOU WATCH FOR MR. FISHER'S NEW MACHINE?
THANKS, MEGAN. CAN YOU GET THE DOOR FOR ME?

I LIKE WAITING.

WELP—THIS IS THE OLD MACHINE. PROB'LY HAS ANOTHER YEAR OR TWO LEFT IN 'ER, BUT YOU KNOW MR. FISHER.
THANKS FOR GETTING THE DOOR.
NEED ANY-THING ELSE?
SURE

MEGAN?! YOU'RE SUPPOSED TO BE WAITING FOR MY NEW MACHINE!!
IT'S OKAY—SHE WAS JUST HELPING ME.
JUST FOR A SECOND.

BOTH OF YOU TO MY OFFICE IMMEDIATELY!!

HE DO THIS A LOT?
YOU GET USED TO IT.
NO TALK-ING!
END

MR. HARRIS? CAN YOU HEAR ME?
UGHH...I MUST'VE HIT MY HEAD...

WH—WHAT WAS I DOING?
IT LOOKED LIKE YOU WERE WHEEL-ING THIS—

—COPY MACHINE?
FRAGILE

YES! YOU WERE WHEELING THIS BRAND-NEW COPY MACHINE TO MISS V'S CLASS!

I—I WAS?
HERE—THIS WAY!
FRAGILE

SPECIAL DELIVERY!

GO TO PAGE 55

HELP OLIVIA WITH THE NEWSPAPER
GO TO PAGE 138

SHARE ENCOUNTER WITH THE MUCK MAN
GO TO PAGE 186

AND NOW THAT YOU HAVE YOUR APOLOGY, YOU CAN BOTH GO— THANKS FOR COMING! GOODBYE!
GRR!
HEY!

PHEW! SO GLAD THAT'S ALL OVER WITH!

HEY! I'M NOT DONE WITH YOU, FISH-MAN! OPEN UP!
QUICK—WE'LL ESCAPE THROUGH THE WINDOW!

AAUGH!
I SEE YOU!!

WE'RE TRAPPED!
FISH-MAN!
WHAT DO WE DO??

LATER
HA HA! YOU'VE GOTTA COME OUT SOME-TIME, FISH-MAN!
I MISS MY FAMILY.
HAW HAW!
THE END

GO TO PAGE 148

HERE!!
I HAVE TO...
UM...
...BATHROOM!
HUFF HUFF HUFF
HE'S GONE.
—HE'S GONE?!
PHEW! THAT WAS CLOSE!
COME ON—LET'S GET BACK TO CLASS!
SOON
?
?
?
YOU CAN MAIL THEM— IT'S LEGAL.
?
GO TO PAGE 89

MITCH, I'M SORRY—

—I HATE TO DO THIS TO YOU, BUT I'VE GOTTA GET BACK TO MISS V'S CLASS.

BUT—THE MUCK MAN! WE'VE ALMOST GOT IT!

I KNOW, BUT I CAN'T STAY AWAY ANY LONGER. THERE WAS THIS WHOLE THING WITH WEIRD RANDALL—
SHH—I'M GOING IN!

GOOD LUCK, MITCH! WHAT A BRAVE SOUL. THERE'S NOTHING SCARIER THAN—

—MR. FISHER!!

GO TO PAGE 74

GO TO PAGE 174

PLUS—I'M SURE SOME PEOPLE HAVE TOYS OR FIDGETS AND THINGS THEY COULD DONATE TO SELL.

HMM...THAT'S NOT A BAD IDEA...

...I COULD GET IN A LOT OF TROUBLE FOR HELPING YOU WITH YOUR IDEA...

FLY THE DRONE AROUND SO THAT MITCH CAN SEE US!
ON IT!
HURRY!

OKAY, WE'RE MOVING!

IT ISN'T WORKING—
HE'S NOT LOOKING!
GO FASTER! FASTER!!

HUMMMM MMMM MMM MMMM
OH NO!
MY NOTE!!

WHERE'D IT GO?!
I DON'T KNOW—
I'M LOOKING!!

?
GO TO PAGE 41

OPEN NOTE
GO TO PAGE 183

TAKE CHARGER
GO TO PAGE 102

GO TO PAGE 223

WEIRD RANDALL—I'M SORRY, BUT THERE'S NO WAY YOU WENT TO ALL THOSE DIFFERENT PLACES.

YOU FOLLOWED ME TO CLASS! **RE-MEMBER**?

STOP WEIRD RANDALL
GO TO PAGE 54

FOLLOW WEIRD RANDALL
GO TO PAGE 3

GO TO PAGE 220

OKAY, MEGAN—ROB AND MITCH HAVE DONE THEIR PARTS—NOW IT'S ALL UP TO YOU.
HUP!

HI, MRS. GLADSTONE! CAN YOU MAKE ONE HUNDRED COPIES OF THIS? IT'S FOR MISS V—SHE'S IN A HURRY!
OF COURSE—BRING IT IN!

HEY, IS THAT A DRONE?
OH—THIS? NO, THIS IS A, UM...

...IT'S NOT A DRONE.
OH! OKAY.
COPY
COPY
COPY
COPY
COPY
COPY
NICE! GOOD COVER, MEGAN.

HERE YOU GO—ONE HUNDRED COPIES.
THANKS!
HEY—THAT LOOKS LIKE MR. FISH—

BYE!
!

PHEW! THAT WAS CLOSE!
HUFF
HUFF

GO TO PAGE 18

I'M SO HUNGRY FROM WORKING SO HARD—AND NOW IT'S ALL RUINED!!

WAIT A SEC—THIS IS AN ESSAY ON NEUROSCIENCE! IT'S BRILLIANT!
ACTUALLY, IT'S AN IN-DEPTH OVERVIEW OF EMERGING NEUROTECHNOLOGIES—

—SPECIFICALLY WITHIN IMPLANTABLE BRAIN-MACHINE INTERFACES.
THIS HITS THE SPOT!
OH! TYLER WROTE BACK—HE SAYS THE METEOR RACE IS HIS FAVORITE PART.
NO WAY! THAT'S, LIKE, THE BEST PART! HA HA!

I'M TAKING THESE NIGHT CLASSES FOR COLLEGE AND NEED TO TURN IN A SCIENCE ESSAY...
SO...HUNGRY...

I'LL TRADE YOU SOME FRESH PIZZA FOR YOUR ESSAY.
GO TO PAGE 209

THAT MADE ME AND MELVIN ITCHY, BUT I TOLD HIM THAT I WOULD ALWAYS PROTECT HIM.

WAIT!! YOU WERE TALKING TO MELVIN? **THAT MEANS HE WAS HERE!** WHERE'D YOU PUT HIM?!

GO TO PAGE 207

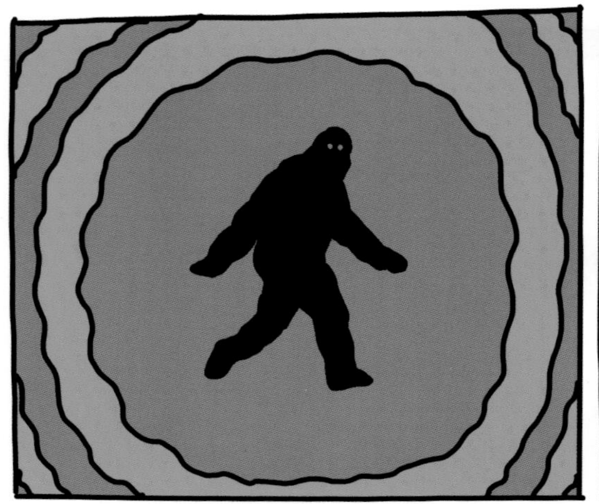

GO TO PAGE 164

HEY, THANKS FOR LETTING ME HELP—NOW I WON'T FAIL!

LATER
JEROME?!
NEED A RIDE?

JEROME—ARE YOU FEELING OKAY? YOU'RE ACTING FUNNY.
MEGAN—THERE'S SOME-THING I HAVE TO TELL YOU...

...I'M GLAD YOU'RE MY SISTER AND I LOVE YOU.
WHAT?! WHAT'S GOTTEN INTO YOU?!

UGH! YOU'RE RIGHT—THIS IS WEIRD! THIS STUPID ADVICE COLUMN DOESN'T KNOW WHAT IT'S TALKING ABOUT! UGH!

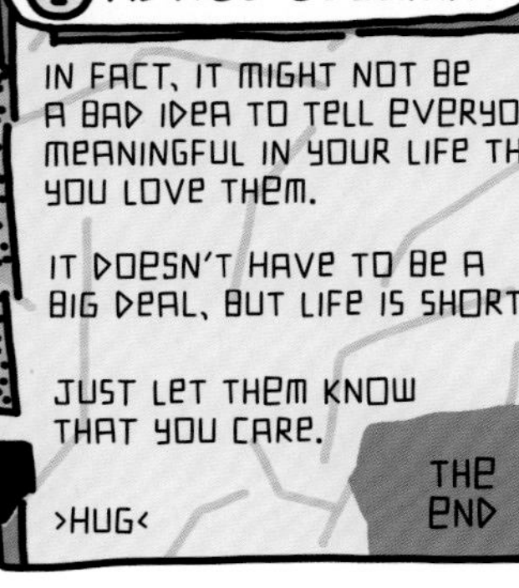
SUNBRIGHT
ADVICE COLUMN?
IN FACT, IT MIGHT NOT BE A BAD IDEA TO TELL EVERYONE MEANINGFUL IN YOUR LIFE THAT YOU LOVE THEM.
IT DOESN'T HAVE TO BE A BIG DEAL, BUT LIFE IS SHORT.
JUST LET THEM KNOW THAT YOU CARE.
>HUG<
THE END

GO TO PAGE 216

I'M TELLING YOU...
WHEE!!
...I'VE NEVER SEEN THEM WORK SO HARD...
HA HA HA
...SEE?

!!

OH! WELL, THEY MUST BE WORN OUT FROM ALL THAT EFFORT... WE'LL JUST HAVE TO FINISH THE PAPER ANOTHER TIME.
HEY, I KNOW THIS MOVIE—

—THE TRAILER ACTUALLY LOOKED PRETTY GOOD.
OH?
AND LOOK—POPCORN!!
SO
THE END

HUH? WHO SAID THAT?!

WELL? WHO WAS IT?

IT WAS ME, MR. FISHER. I WROTE THE ADVICE COLUMN. I'M PREPARED TO PAY FOR IT.

DILLON PEPPER? I MUST SAY, I'M SURPRISED—I WOULDN'T HAVE THOUGHT YOU CAPABLE OF SOMETHING THIS...THIS...DISRESPECTFUL.
WINK!

TO MY OFFICE, MR. PEPPER!!
YES, MR. FISHER.

DILLON...HE... HE SAVED ME.

I THINK SOMEONE LIKES YOU!
MY HERO!
THE END

GO TO PAGE 112

OH, FINE—
LET'S DO IT.
GET TACOS?!

WHAT? NO—I'LL HELP WITH THE OPINION SECTION.
OH.

IS THAT OKAY, MISS V?
JUST BE SURE TO FINISH BE-FORE THE BELL.
YES! THANK YOU!

I THINK I'M GONNA WRITE ABOUT HOW WREKKER IS THE BEST MOBILE GAME.
IT'S NOT—WAR BATTLE IS THE BEST!

THAT'S COOL—I'M JUST WRITING ABOUT MY OPINION.
PFFT!
YOUR OPINION IS DUMB!

HA HA! MAYBE YOU COULD WRITE YOUR OWN OPINION COLUMN?
YEAH, SCOTT!
YEAH!

GO TO PAGE 35

GO TO PAGE 221

NONONONO, WE'RE GOING ABOUT THIS ALL WRONG!

WE NEED TO START FROM THE BEGINNING!
GET YOUR PHONES OUT—READY?
RECORDING?
I SUPPOSE I'LL START WITH MY GRANDFATHER—ARCHIBALD FISHER...

GRANDPA ARCHIE WAS THE FIRST SUNBRIGHT MIDDLE SCHOOL PRINCIPAL.

SUNBRIGHT
MY FATHER—HENRY FISHER—CONTINUED GRANDPA ARCHIE'S LEGACY AS SUNBRIGHT MIDDLE'S SECOND PRINCIPAL.

AS YOU CAN SEE, I COME FROM A LONG AND ELITE LINE OF PRINCIPALS...
STILL RECORDING?
UGH
WHEN DOES THE NEXT PROJECT START?
THE END

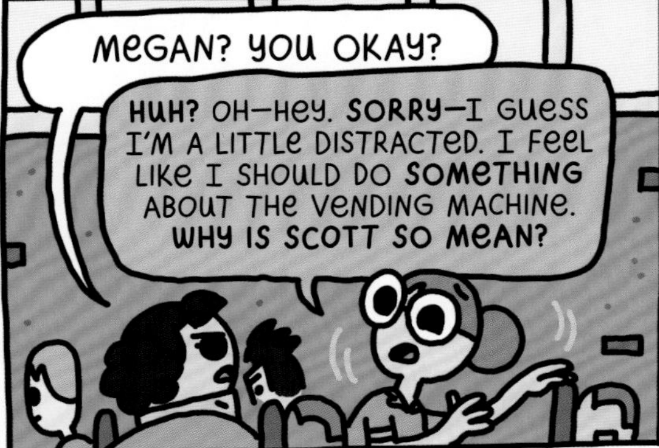

OLIVIA—THAT'S IT!! WE CAN SELL THE NEWSPAPER IN THE VENDING MACHINE TO MAKE THE MONEY NEEDED TO BUY NEW SNACKS!

GO TO PAGE 87

UGH! FINALLY!
SHEESH!
HE'S SO CRUEL!
HEY!
SEND MEGAN TO MY OFFICE IF YOU FIND HER!
HE'S BACK!

WE HEARD YOU THE FIRST TIME!

THINK HE'S ACTUALLY GONE THIS TIME?
HRF!
BETTER BE.

I CAN'T HOLD IT ANY-MORE!!
GOOD JOB, ROB!
HA HA!
WHONK!

CLICK!

GO TO PAGE 80

PART 2 ON PAGE 75

LET'S SEE IF WE CAN FIND SOME NIBBLES...
F33
LET'S

...HEY—MAYBE WEIRD RANDALL WILL GIVE YOU ONE OF HIS POTATOES!
HA HA
HA HA

SO—YOU MUST'VE SNEAKED INTO MY BACKPACK AT HOME.
YOU CUTE LITTLE SNEAK!

IT'S A GOOD THING I CAUGHT YOU BEFORE SCOTT VILE DID. I DON'T WANT TO THINK WHAT HE MIGHT—

AAAAAAAAAH!!
VINCENT!

NOT AGAIN!!
GO TO PAGE 171

GO TO PAGE 200

YOU'VE **GOT** THIS.
YOU CAN **DO** IT.

RUN AS FAST AS YOU CAN—YOU'LL BE SAFE INSIDE.
SUNBRIGHT

NOW!!
HUFF
HUFF
HUFF

HELP!!!
?
AWK!
SKRAW!

SHOO!
GO ON!
GET!
SKIPPING CLASS **AND** LITTERING!
I SHOULDN'T HAVE LEFT MITCH!
THE END

HOLD UP YOUR COMICS ONCE YOU'VE FINISHED!

GOOD, GOOD, GOOD...
I GOT 'EM! I'VE GOT THE KEYS!

THANKS, MISS V! LET'S STOCK THE MACHINE!
IT WENT JUST AS I DREAMED IT WOULD... ONLY MUCH BETTER!
RRRINGG!
?
?
QUICK—PUT THE COMICS IN SO PEOPLE CAN BUY THEM ON THEIR WAY TO CLASS! GO! GO!!
I'M HURRYING!

WAIT—WHAT'S HAPPENING? I CAN'T SEE!
TOO...MANY... PEOPLE...
HEY—ARE THOSE MITCH COMICS?!
WHERE?
I WANT ONE!
ME TOO!

GO TO PAGE 10

GO TO PAGE 105

AND WELCOME EVERYONE TO OUR NEW UNIT—
READY FOR IT?
—OUR CLASS NEWSPAPER!

LET'S GET STARTED!

CAN'T WE, LIKE, MAKE AN APP INSTEAD???
UGH

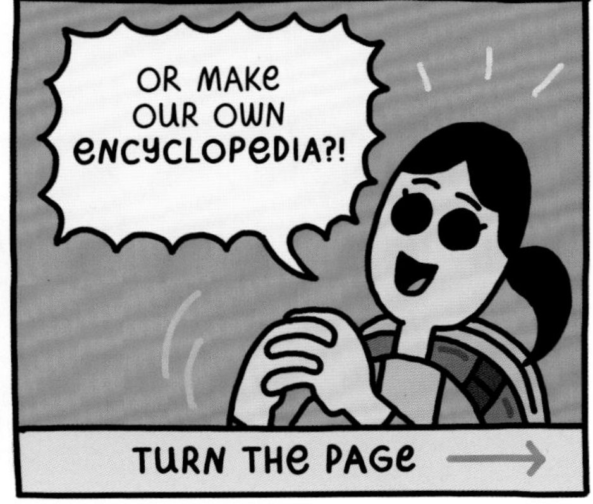

RAISE HAND GO TO PAGE 114
DON'T RAISE HAND GO TO PAGE 230

HOLD IT...
?
?

...THERE'S MY NEW COPIER!!
UM...
UH-OH!

UM—HEY, MR. FISHER!
?
WE WERE JUST—UH—TESTING IT FOR YOU.

IS THAT RIGHT? **WELL??** LET'S SEE WHAT IT CAN DO!
OH, I'M PRETTY SURE WE DON'T NEED TO CHECK, MR. FISHER.
—HEY!
STEAL
I CAN'T WAIT TO SEE YOU ALL IN TROUBLE—

DELIVERY FOR TODD?
PIZZA'S HERE!
GO TO PAGE 190

MITCH IS RIGHT—WITH ALL THE MOVIE REVIEWS AND GAMES, THIS REALLY WILL BE THE BEST!! HA HA!

SORRY TO INTERRUPT, BUT WILL THERE STILL BE ENOUGH ROOM TO INCLUDE MY ESSAY?

SPEAKING OF MY ESSAY—TO WHICH STYLE DO YOU PREFER I ADHERE?
TURABIAN? MLA? I CAN DO APA...
OH! AND SHOULD I INCLUDE A BIBLIOGRAPHY?

CAN YOU GUYS KEEP IT DOWN A BIT? WE'RE TRYING TO CONCENTRATE.

WHERE'D ALL THOSE SCREENS COME FROM?
SHH!!

OH, GOOD—THEY ALL SEEM TO BE HARD AT WORK! THEY WON'T MISS ME IF I STEP AWAY FOR A LITTLE LONGER...
WAIT—SO HE'S A SPY?
SHE'S A SPY—

HE'S HIM IN THE FUTURE.
THE FUTURE...

GO TO PAGE 76

YOU WANT ME TO STAND HERE...
AND WAIT...
UNTIL IT COMES?

SORRY, MR. FISHER— SOUNDS LIKE IT COULD TAKE A WHILE...
I'VE GOTTA GET TO CLASS— TODAY'S OUR NEWSPAPER PROJECT!

DID YOU SAY...NEWSPAPER?

NEWSPAPER DAY WAS EVERY DAY BACK WHEN I WAS YOUR AGE!!
OKAY—BYE, MR. FISHER!

YOU KIDS CAN LOOK AT YOUR PHONES AT ANY TIME TO READ NEWS FROM ALL AROUND THE WORLD...

...BUT MY GENERATION HAD TO WAIT! WAIT FOR THE NEWSPAPER!!
HRM... THAT DOES NOT SOUND LIKE FUN.

GO TO PAGE 17

STAY BACK—
THIS COULD GET
DANGEROUS.
CREAK!
?
?
?
RUN
GO TO PAGE 225
STAY
GO TO PAGE 9

NAME IDEAS FOR THE PAPER? I BET WE CAN THINK OF A GOOD ONE...
SUNBRIGHT CENTRAL!
NEW NEWS!
THE SCHOOL JOURNAL!
LET'S COME BACK TO A NAME.
OH!!
CHECK THIS OUT...
[HEADER]
[SUBHEADER]
[ARTICLE TITLE]
[BODY TEXT]
[IMAGE]
[CAPTION]
[CALEN-DAR]
[EVENTS]
...IT'S MY DESIGN TEMPLATE! WE JUST ADD OUR OWN PICS AND ARTICLES AND WHATEVER.
I LOVE IT!
WHAT IF WE PUT GAMES IN THE PAPER? LIKE A WORD SEARCH OR A MAZE OR SOME-THING LIKE THAT?
WAIT—I COULD TOTALLY DO FILM REVIEWS! I HAVE A BUNCH OF STREAMING SERVICES AND I CAN JUST WATCH IN CLASS AT 2x SPEED ON MY LAPTOP!
I LOVE THE IDEA, BUT THE PAPER IS DUE TODAY.
THAT'S ONLY ENOUGH TIME FOR ONE MOVIE!
GO TO PAGE 11

IN FACT, I SAVED UP ENOUGH MONEY TO BUY MY OWN NEWSPAPER SUBSCRIPTION!!

GO TO PAGE 77

GO TO PAGE 181

THAT'S RIGHT—TODAY'S THE LAST DAY TO TURN IN ANY LATE WORK.
YOU'RE LETTING THEM DO MITCH'S HOME-WORK FOR HIM?!

BUT WE HAD TO WRITE AND MAIL ALL THOSE LETTERS TO STUDENTS AT OTHER SCHOOLS—
—PLUS WE HAD TO REPLY TO ALL THE LETTERS OUR PEN PALS WROTE TO US!

THERE'S NOT ENOUGH TIME TO DO IT ALL IN ONE DAY!
WELL, NO— IT'S PRACTICALLY IMPOSSIBLE...
WITHOUT A DRONE!
DRONE

IT'S FAST!
SPEED!
IT CAN FLIP!
AND IT'S QUIET!

I COULD USE IT TO FLY MITCH'S LETTERS TO AN-OTHER SCHOOL!
CAN WE, MISS V?
PLEASE?
HMM...

...JUST DON'T LET MR. FISHER CATCH US.
YES!!

GO TO PAGE 43

OH MY GASP—IS THAT IT? THE ACTUAL SUNBRIGHT MUCK MAN?! IT'S JUST AROUND THE CORNER!
IT'S NEAR THE GYM.
SO TAKE A PICTURE AND LET'S GET OUT OF HERE!
THIS IS SUPER CREEPY!
NOT YET— I NEED A BETTER SHOT...
THERE ARE LOTS OF DARK AND BLURRY PHOTOS OF THE MUCK MAN—I WANNA GET A GOOD ONE.
LOOK! IT WENT INSIDE THE LOCKER ROOM!
STAY WITH MITCH
GO TO PAGE 229
LEAVE MITCH
GO TO PAGE 121

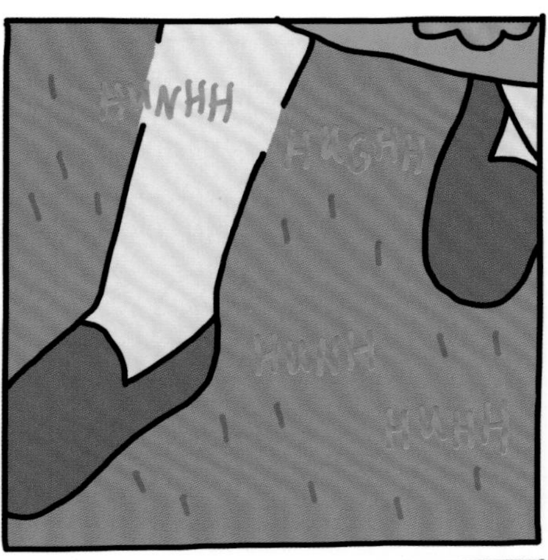

GO TO PAGE 146

UM...
WHY ARE ALL YOUR STUDENTS LYING ON THE FLOOR LIKE THAT?
HAVE YOU CALLED THE **NURSE**?
I'M CALLING THE NURSE.
I—I DON'T KNOW...

NURSE JACKIE?
HELP!!
COME QUICK!

DON'T WORRY, NURSE JACKIE—
—WHOOPS!

BONK!
CLONK!

MISS VALENTINE?!
DON'T WORRY—
I'M COMING!

GASP! DON'T WORRY, MISS V—I HAVE **TRAINED FOR THIS VERY MOMENT!**
UGH...WHAT HAPPENED?

NEVER MIND **THAT**—
HELP ME GET SOME **TOWELS AND BANDAGES!**
O—KAY?
THE END

GO TO PAGE 101

NOW, OVER HERE—THIS IS WHAT I WANT TO SHOW YOU...

THE FIRST ISSUE OF THE SUNBRIGHT GAZETTE—STARTED BY ERASTUS R. FISHER.
THE SUNBRIGHT GAZETTE
THE STUDENT SITUATION: A PROPOSAL FOR PROGRESS
A MESSAGE FROM YOUR EDITOR-IN-CHIEF E.R.

WAIT—SO THERE USED TO BE A NEWSPAPER FOR THE WHOLE SCHOOL?
WELL—ONE ISSUE, AT LEAST.

NO ONE WANTED TO READ ABOUT CLASS ASSIGNMENTS OR FISHER'S ARTICLE "WHEN I'M PRINCIPAL."
HEE HEE!!

I WAS HIS TEACHER. DID YOU KNOW THAT?
YOU WERE MR. FISHER'S TEACHER?!

HA HA! YES—I TAUGHT ENGLISH. OF COURSE, THAT WAS SO VERY LONG AGO...
THAT'S ACTUALLY KIND OF COOL!
GO TO PAGE 180

NO—NONE OF THE PICTURES TURNED OUT, SO I CHANGED MY WHOLE REPORT.
OH NO. I'M SO SORRY.
BUT—IF YOU COULDN'T WRITE ABOUT THE MUCK MAN, WHAT'S YOUR REPORT ABOUT?

WAIT—IS THIS **ME**?
IT'S TITLED **"MY FRIEND MEGAN: MUCK MAN HUNTER."** I WROTE AND DREW IT WHILE YOU WERE SLEEPING.

NO WAY! HA! HA! I'VE NEVER BEEN IN A **NEWSPAPER** BEFORE!
HERE...

THESE WERE THE LAST TWO IN THE MACHINE. I'LL READ YOU MY ARTICLE UNTIL YOUR RIDE COMES.
AW, MITCH—YOU'RE THE BEST!
KSH!
THE END

THAT'S IT—I'M TELLING MR. FISHER!
WAIT—NO!!

TELL PRINCIPAL WALTHAM—MR. FISHER'S AFRAID.
MR. H?

REALLY? MR. FISHER'S AFRAID OF SCOTT VILE?
AND HIS DAD.
HA
HA

HA HA HA! WAIT—FOR REALSIES? I CAN'T TELL IF YOU'RE JOKING.
REALLY! FISHER WENT TO SCHOOL WITH SCOTT'S DAD. IT'S, LIKE, A WHOLE THING.

I'D LOVE TO HEAR ALL ABOUT IT SOMEDAY FROM FISHER!
HA HA
HA
HA
HA HA

OKAY, THEN—GUESS I'LL TELL PRINCIPAL WALTHAM.

GO TO PAGE 12

I MEAN, IT DOESN'T **HAVE** TO BE MITCH—WE COULD INTERVIEW THE ART TEACHER?
HMM?

DILLON...

UH, **YEAH**—IT'S ME. DILLON. HA HA.

I MEAN, YOU COULD JUST **DO IT ALONE,** IF YOU WANT? I DON'T HAVE TO BE THERE. IS THAT WHAT YOU WANT?
UH-HUH...WHAT-EVER YOU SAY...

OH! OKAY. I GUESS I'LL DO MY OWN THING. **GOOD LUCK!**
!

LOVESTRUCK! GO TO PAGE 89

WELL, YOU MUST'VE DONE SOMETHING FOR THE SCREEN TO SUDDENLY TURN BLACK!
BUT I DIDN'T! WAIT—HOLD ON...

...IT'S THE DRONE BATTERIES—THEY MUST BE OUT OF POWER!!
BUT THE DRONE'S BY MR. FISHER'S OFFICE—WHAT DO WE DO?

UM, MISS V? CAN I GO TO THE BATHROOM?
AND STOP DISTRACTING THE CLASS FROM THEIR ASSIGNMENTS? YES! PLEASE, PLEASE GO.

AND ME, MISS V? PLEASE?
BE QUICK—WE'LL HAVE TO PRINT OUR PAPER SOON.

THIS IS YOUR PLAN?! YOUR DRONE DIES AND YOUR PLAN IS TO TAKE A BATHROOM BREAK?!
SHH—WE'RE NOT GOING TO THE BATHROOM...

...WE'RE GOING TO RESCUE MY DRONE!!
GO TO PAGE 52

...I OWE ROB A NEW TROMBONE.
WHAT—WHY?
GASP!
DID YOU YARK IN MY TROMBONE?!

...AND, MISS V?
Y-YES?
YOU'RE GONNA WANT A NEW COPY MACHINE.

OH? OH! WELL, LET'S JUST, UM...
I'M SORRY.
OOG.
BUT—WHAT ABOUT OUR LYRICS?!
R.I.P.

EVERYONE JUST CALM DOWN—WE'LL TRY AGAIN NEXT CLASS.
WEIRD RANDALL?
HELLO.

MMM—DID SOME-ONE MAKE SOUP?
UM... THAT'S NOT SOUP.
I THINK I'M GONNA BE SICK...
THE END

I'M SURE MR. H HAS ENOUGH TO DO—BESIDES, THIS'LL BE A FUN PROJECT!

OKAY—STEP ONE...
PSH!

INSTRUCTIONS ARE FOR WEAKLINGS. I'LL SHOW YOU HOW IT'S DONE!

I'M GONNA NEED TOOLS AND A FEW PEOPLE WILLING TO GET A LITTLE DIRTY.

I SAID I NEED TOOLS!!
UM, I DON'T THINK THOSE ARE SUPPOSED TO GO TOGETHER.

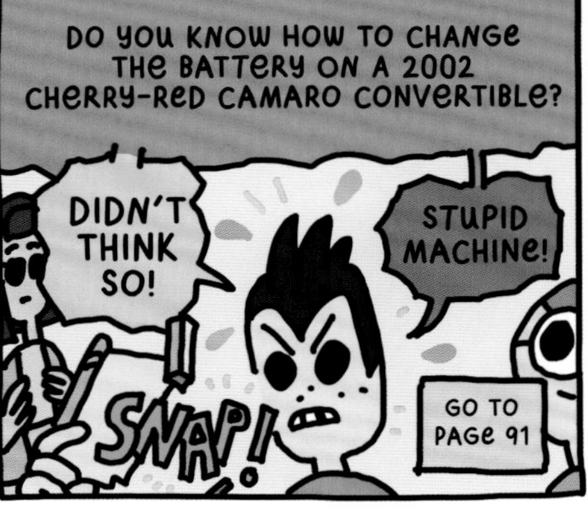
DO YOU KNOW HOW TO CHANGE THE BATTERY ON A 2002 CHERRY-RED CAMARO CONVERTIBLE?
DIDN'T THINK SO!
STUPID MACHINE!
SNAP!
GO TO PAGE 91

WHUNK!

WHACK!!

BOONK!

!

DUNK!

GLK!

PWANG!

PONK!

GO TO PAGE 85

HUFF HUFF

VINCENT! COME BACK!
IT'S >HUFF< JUST >HUFF< ME!

VINCENT!

HEY!

HUNHH

STOP!
FFHUFF

HUHH
HUHH
HUAAUGH!

GO TO PAGE 67

STUDENTS HAVE BEEN SEND-ING ME THEIR QUESTIONS AND PROBLEMS ON THE SCHOOL'S **ME PAGE**, BUT THERE ARE TOO MANY! I CANT ANSWER EVERYONE IN TIME!!

A QUESTION ABOUT LOVE GO TO PAGE 62	**A QUESTION ABOUT CAREER** GO TO PAGE 28

!

MEGAN! FINALLY! WHAT TOOK YOU SO LONG? I WISH YOU HAD A **PHONE**!

HA HA, TELL ME ABOUT IT!
I'M AFRAID YOU'RE **TOO LATE TO CONTRIBUTE**—I'M ABOUT TO PRINT OUR NEWSPAPER.

PERFECT! **PRINT IT ON THIS!**
WHOA—IS THAT **SPECIAL** PAPER?
WHERE'D YOU GET IT?!

IT'S **NEWSPRINT**—MRS. BIRMINGHAM GAVE IT TO ME. OH—AND SHE TOLD ME **ALL** ABOUT MR. FISHER! **HA HA!**
STOP THE PRESSES AND TELL US **EVERYTHING**!

OH, I WILL!
THE END

WAIT—WHY ARE YOU HERE?

OKAY—RANDALL? CAN YOU GO BACK TO YOUR OWN CLASS NOW?

MELVIN WANTS TO STAY.

MELVIN? WHO IS MELVIN?
DO YOU MEAN RANDALL?
DOES RANDALL WANT TO STAY?

MISS V?

—SIGH—
YES, TINA?
GO TO PAGE 96

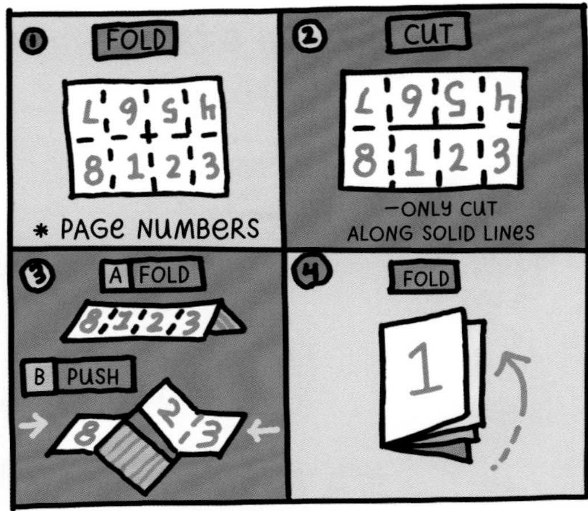

GO TO PAGE 129

STEP #4,728

NOW GIVE MR. FISHER AN ANGRY FACE LIKE THESE:

FACT: MR. Fisher is always angry because his breath stinks.

BONUS FACT: Mr. Fisher is always sweaty and he stinks (see fact above).

HOW TO DRAW MR. FISHER

BY: mitch

PART 2

MR. FISHER CATCHPHRASES:

I STINK!

EW

YOCK

I GROSS

DUHH

I'M MAD!

I'M the BOSS.

GAS

MORE GAS

YORE IN TRUBBEL!

WHOT'S THAT STINK? OH WAIT—IT'S ME.

TURN TO PAGE 184

LUNCH OR AFTER SCHOOL. OKAY—THANKS, MISS V.
I'LL FINISH IT THEN.

LUNCH
ALL RIGHT—LET'S FINISH THIS POEM!
DILLON... DILLON...

...I'VE GOT NOTHING!
SORRY, MEGAN—TIME FOR CLASS. SEE YOU AGAIN AFTER SCHOOL?

AFTER SCHOOL
FILL-IN? WHEELIN'? PENICILLIN?
TAP TAP TAP

I'M AFRAID YOUR TIME'S UP—AND IT LOOKS LIKE YOUR RIDE'S HERE.
I'VE BEEN WAITING FOREVER!
NONONONO!

LATER
TILLON? HILLON? WILLON?
THE END

OKAY.
WELL...
UM...
15

I THINK I'M DONE? HEH.
REALLY?! CAN I SEE?!
I DON'T DRAW A LOT OF REAL PEOPLE...

WELL...
UM...
HERE IT IS.
GOODNESS!
OH
MY
I LOVE IT!
HA HA HA

REALLY?
YOU DON'T THINK IT'S TOO—
LET'S DO THIS INTER-VIEW!
WHAT DO YOU LIKE ABOUT SOCCER?
I DON'T KNOW... IT'S FUN?
GREAT!
WOW— MY FIRST INTER-VIEW!

I HAVE A DELIVERY HERE FOR A TODD?
? ? ?

GO TO PAGE 97

HA! YOU'RE REALLY DOING IT—
A SCHOOL NEWSPAPER!
WELL—
A CLASS PAPER.
HA!
STUDENTS, FORGET YOUR OTHER CLASSES— THIS IS IMPORTANT!
NOBODY LEAVES UNTIL THE PAPER IS COMPLETE.

MR. FISHER—THAT'S NOT NECESSARY—
HA
NON-SENSE!

I'M HAPPY TO HELP- MORE THAN HAPPY! HA HA!
NOW—WE'LL HAVE TO START AT ONCE!

WELL?! DON'T JUST SIT THERE—

—THERE'S SO MUCH TO DO!
I'LL NEED TO WRITE A WELCOME MESSAGE!
AND I'LL NEED A PHOTO OF MYSELF AS THE EDITOR IN CHIEF!
LET'S GET TO WORK!
GO TO PAGE 140

I WONDER WHAT IT WAS LIKE FOR YOU TO TEACH MR. FISHER...
ARE YOU OKAY?!
HA HA HA HA
THANK YOU—I REALLY NEEDED A LAUGH! OH, MEGAN, THERE'S SO VERY MUCH TO KNOW ABOUT THIS SCHOOL. WE HAVE MUCH TO DISCUSS—
WE DO?
SUCH AS, WHAT ARE WE GOING TO DO WITH THIS GIANT BOX OF UNUSED NEWSPRINT?
WHY DO YOU HAVE ALL THAT?
OH, ERASTUS SPENT A GOB OF MONEY TO BUY ALL THIS NEWSPRINT FOR FUTURE ISSUES OF THE PAPER THAT WERE NEVER MADE.
OOPS—SOUNDS LIKE MR. FISHER WAS A TROUBLEMAKER! HA HA HA!
IT'S PART OF THE REASON HE WAS HELD BACK A YEAR.
WAIT—WHAT?!
GO TO PAGE 29

DEAR DISRESPECTED,
MR. FISHER IS IN CHARGE AND EVERYONE KNOWS IT. MR. FISHER WENT TO A SPECIAL SCHOOL TO BECOME ASSISTANT PRINCIPAL AND HE DESERVES RESPECT FROM ALL THE STUDENTS. THIS IS OFFICIAL.

GO TO PAGE 98

LEAVE WEIRD RANDALL
GO TO PAGE 106

KEEP FOLLOWING WEIRD RANDALL
GO TO PAGE 69

GO TO PAGE 102

NOW PUT MR. FISHER IN HIS FAVORITE PLACES
THE POOL
i STINK!
EW
YOCK
i GROSS
DUHH
THE TOILET
i'M MAD!
AND THIRSTIE
HOW TO DRAW MR. FISHER
BY: mitch
PART 3
GARBAGE
i'M THE BOSS.
FISH SOUP
GAS
MORE GAS
WHOT'S THAT STINK?
OH WAIT— IT'S ME.
MORE ON PAGE 58

GO TO PAGE 110

CONTINUE HUNTING FOR THE MUCK MAN
GO TO PAGE 113

HELP MITCH ESCAPE MR. FISHER'S OFFICE
GO TO PAGE 22

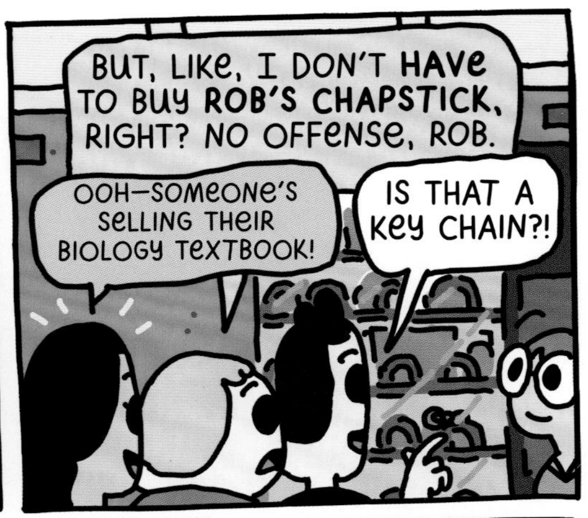

IF IT MAKES A TON OF MONEY, CAN WE BUY A BUNCH OF SUPER-SWANKY SNACKS?

I GUESS, PROBABLY.

GO TO PAGE 71

I'M WARNING YOU, FISH-MAN! OPEN THE DOOR!

WHERE'D THAT APOLOGY GO?

COME ON, COME ON—WHERE ARE YOU?!

GAH! WHY IS THERE SO MUCH TRASH?!

I'M NOT LEAVING UNTIL YOU'VE APOLOGIZED TO ME AND MY SON! GOT IT?!

GO TO PAGE 53

UGH... WHY ISN'T THIS WORKING?
RRINGGG
AND THERE'S THE BELL! TURN IN YOUR ASSIGNED WRITING SO I CAN FINISH OUR NEWSPAPER BY THE NEXT TIME WE MEET.
OH NO!

I'M NOT FINISHED! I STILL NEED A GOOD RHYME FOR DILLON!
BYE, MEGAN!
HEH, BYE...

HEY—YOU COMIN' TO NEXT PERIOD?
OH, UM...

MEGAN? ARE YOU OKAY?
I DIDN'T FINISH WRITING MY POEM!
TXT
TXT

IT WON'T MAKE THE PAPER IN TIME, BUT YOU CAN COME BACK AT LUNCH OR AFTER SCHOOL TO FINISH AND GET A GRADE.
NOT A BIG DEAL.
GO TO PAGE 177

THANKS—I'M STARVING!
THAT COMES OUT TO ELEVEN BUCKS.
OH! UM...

...ANYONE HAVE ELEVEN BUCKS I CAN BORROW?
HERE—THESE ARE ALL READY TO GO.
?

NOW THIS IS REALLY AN ACCOMPLISHMENT!
HA HA!

UM...MR. FISHER?
Original Sunbright newspaper staff
UH-OH!
WHAT ELSE IS IN YOUR PAPER??
PLEASE DON'T OPEN UP THE PAPER!
IT'S TOO LATE—I ALREADY PRINTED EVERYTHING!!
HUH? WHAT'S INSIDE?

THERE'S NOTHING IN HERE! IT'S BLANK INSIDE!
PHEW!
NOT SO EASY TO USE A COPIER, IS IT? HA HA!

HERE...I'LL TAKE CARE OF THE PIZZA AND ORDER MORE—TWO LARGE JALAPEÑO, PLEASE.
O...KAY?
EW!
NOW, LET'S TAKE A LOOK AT THIS COPIER...
THE END

KNOCK ON THE WINDOW	FLY AROUND
GO TO PAGE 36	GO TO PAGE 124

GO TO PAGE 160

GO TO PAGE 201

MR. FISHER'S VACATION
PART TWO
A "MR. FISHER COMIC STORY" BY MITCH
HAY. YOU KIDS!
I'M IN CHORG!
MAKE ME A SANDCASTLE!
DO IT! NOW!
BIGGER! MAKE ME MY THRONE!
I AM KING!
LUNCH!
EAT!
YAY!
EW! TOO STINKY!
SPIT!
?
READ MORE ON PAGE 205

FREE MITCH GO TO PAGE 104

STOP THE PROTEST GO TO PAGE 162

GO TO PAGE 107

COME ON, ROB—RUN!!
UM...

Hey!!
YOINK!

SHOCK!

HA HA! STILL GOT IT!

NOW...LET'S TAKE A LITTLE WALK TO MY OFFICE, SHALL WE?
BUT, MR. FISHER—
—SHE'S SHOCKED STIFF!!

NOT A PROBLEM!
HELP!
THE END

BUT, MISS V—I WAS HELPING WEIRD RANDALL! AND MITCH!

THAT'S GOOD OF YOU TO HELP YOUR FRIENDS, BUT WE STILL NEED YOU TO WRITE SOMETHING FOR OUR CLASS PAPER. MEGAN?
SIGH

BUT TEN MINUTES? THAT'S NOT ENOUGH TIME TO EVEN DO ANYTHING.
WRITE WRITE

WELL, YOU CAN AT LEAST TRY TO DO WHAT YOU CAN WITH THE TIME YOU HAVE...

...OR YOU CAN GIVE UP NOW AND KNOW THAT YOU'VE FAILED.

HMPH! IT'S NOT EVEN FAIR!
TRY GO TO PAGE 51
GIVE UP GO TO PAGE 172

FIND MR. H FOR HELP

GO TO PAGE 45

FIND MONEY TO BUY AND RESCUE VINCENT

GO TO PAGE 64

I SHOULD SEND YOU TO MY OFFICE FOR THE DAY AND CALL YOUR PARENTS.

NO! PLEASE, MR. FISHER—WE WERE JUST GOING BACK TO CLASS. RIGHT, WEIRD RANDALL?

MR. BIGGER	MRS. BIGGER	THEIR BABY
GO TO PAGE 212	GO TO PAGE 139	GO TO PAGE 19

WAIT. JAVI—WHAT IF I INTERVIEWED YOU FOR THE PAPER?

SERIOUSLY?!
I'VE NEVER BEEN IN THE NEWS BEFORE!

HEY, JAVI—
CAN I TAKE PICTURES?
I'LL GET MY SOCCER BALL FROM MY LOCKER!
THIS IS SO COOL!
HA HA HA
HA HA HA
15

WHAT THE—
MY PHONE JUST DIED!

THAT'S OKAY, GEM—
HEY!
?
—ANYONE HAVE A CHARGER THAT SHE CAN USE?
HA HA HA
HA
MISS V KEEPS ONE IN HER DRAWER—
—UNLESS YOU'RE TOO CHICKEN TO LOOK!
HA HA HA
HA
HA
OPEN DRAWER GO TO PAGE 125
DON'T LOOK GO TO PAGE 95

MEGAN—LISTEN TO ME. YOU DON'T KNOW SCOTT'S FATHER LIKE I DO. YOU DON'T KNOW WHAT HE'LL DO TO ME!!
DO TO YOU?
YOU THINK SCOTT'S A BULLY? WELL, WHO DO YOU THINK HE LEARNED IT FROM? HUH?
YOU HAVE TO MAKE THIS APOLOGY COUNT!
HE'LL BE HERE SOON—IT MUST BE FINISHED BY HIS ARRIVAL!
BETTER YET—WE'LL MAIL IT! HA HA! YES—WE'LL MAKE THE APOLOGY AND AVOID SEEING SCOTT'S FATHER ALTOGETHER! HA!
I SAID HE'S ON HIS WAY! HE'S GONNA POUND BOTH OF YOU!
ARE YOU DONE?
ALMOST...
SLAM!
GASP! DID YOU HEAR THAT?
FINALLY.
OHNONONO...
HE'S HERE!!
GO TO PAGE 79

SNIFF!
MEREDITH?
DANCE DANCE HAPPY DANCE
—IS EVERYTHING OKAY IN HERE?
OLIVER! I MEAN— MR. TWEED!
SNIFF
I—
I THOUGHT I HEARD—
I MEAN—
I DIDN'T MEAN TO INTERRUPT—
HERE—THIS IS FOR YOU.
BYE!
M
THANK
YOU?
ce ce
OH MY GOSH
SNIFF
DOES IT LOOK LIKE I'VE BEEN CRYING?
NO—NOT AT ALL, MISS V!
YOU LOOK GREAT! HEH.

GO TO PAGE 59

WHAT AM I SUPPOSED TO—

GASP!
IS THAT JEROME?

HA! IT IS! JEROME!
HUH? IT WASN'T ME!

JEROME—DO YOU HAVE THE CAR?
I DROVE HERE. WHAT DO YOU THINK?
YAY!
OKAY, JEROME. MR. H—I NEED YOUR HELP.
?

SO

THEN
AHH...IT'S SO NICE TO BE HOME AND TOGETHER AGAIN!
THE END

MR. FISHER'S VACATION PART 3

A "MR. FISHER COMIC STORY" BY MITCH

MORE ON PAGE 16

TOTALLY!
WHAT'S THE TUNE?
OH! UM...

...CAN I PLAY IT, MISS V? IN CLASS?
OF COURSE! WHAT A GREAT IDEA!

UGH.
NO ONE WANTS TO LISTEN TO A DUMB OL' TROMBONE.

WHY CAN'T YOU PLAY SOMETHING COOL? LIKE DRUMS OR GUITAR?

CAN YOU PLAY THE TROMBONE, SCOTT?

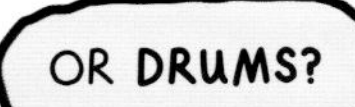
OR DRUMS?

OR THE GUITAR?

PSH! I DON'T HAVE TIME TO—

BRONK!
!
!
!

GO TO PAGE 21

I PUT HIM IN MY EAR.
...AND?
OH—I PUT HIM IN MY OTHER EAR. HI!
IT WAS INSIDE YOUR EAR THIS ENTIRE TIME?!?
LOOK, MEGAN—MELVIN WANTS TO SAY HI TO—
I FOLLOWED YOU ALL THE WAY AROUND THE SCHOOL AND LISTENED TO YOU TALK ON AND ON...
...AND NOW YOU'RE TELLING ME THAT THE LITTLE PIECE OF GUM THAT YOU WERE MISSING WAS IN YOUR EAR THIS WHOLE—
OH, HEY—
MEGAN!
DILLON! HI! HA HA! EXCUSE ME A MOMENT...
OH! OKAY.

GO TO PAGE 31

GO TO PAGE 166

YOU MEAN YOU'D PAY ME FOR MY WORK? IN SLICES OF PIZZA?!
OH MY GOSH. YOU'RE RIGHT—THAT DOES SOUND INSULTING! I SWEAR I DIDN'T MEAN—
DO YOU HAVE VEGGIE OPTIONS?
WAIT—ARE YOU SERIOUS?
I ALREADY DID THE RESEARCH—REWRITING IT'LL BE A BREEZE!
NOW—WHERE'S THAT PIZZA?
HOW COME TINA GETS PIZZA?!
YEAH! I WANT SOME, TOO.
AND ME!
MITCH'S PEN PAL IS MY NEW BFF!
ALL REQUIRED CORRESPONDENCE HAS BEEN MET FOR THE ASSIGNMENT. CONGRATULATIONS, EVERYONE—YOU'VE EARNED MITCH AN A!
HOORAY!
OKAY—NOW ASK WHAT KIND OF MUSIC HE LIKES!
AND FOOD!
AND SHOWS!
OH, MITCH...
...I HOPE YOU'RE OKAY...
...AND THAT'S WHY I ORGANIZE EMAILS THIS WAY!
Z
THE END

HELP OPEN WEIRD RANDALL'S MAIL
GO TO PAGE 44

PLUG IN THE COPY MACHINE
GO TO PAGE 39

THWONK!

SOON, IN MR. FISHER'S OFFICE
MY...MY PIZZA...
OLMP!
NOM!

HEY—YOU STILL OWE ME ELEVEN DOLLARS, PLUS TIP!
SO, SO HUNGRY.

WHY AM I EVEN HERE?
I'M WORK-ING.

I DIDN'T EVEN GO TO SCHOOL HERE!! CAN I CALL MY BOSS?!
QUIET—I'M EATING!
I'VE HAD A VERY STRESS-FUL DAY!
THE END

OKAY, UM—**MISTER**?
WHAT?
BZZT!

UM—IS IT **MR. BIGGER**?
MY NAME IS FISHER—MR. FISHER. ARE YOU FEELING OKAY?
UM...
FLIP!

...I FEEL **FINE**, MR. FISHER. I WAS JUST **ANSWERING** THE **QUESTION** YOU ASKED.

WHAT DID YOU **SAY**? **I** ASK THE QUESTIONS AROUND HERE! **GOT IT**?
?
TXT
TXT
TXT

YES, MR. FISHER. OF COURSE, BUT—
TXT
TXT

HOW **LONG** UNTIL THEY **RESPECT ME**???
?
GO TO PAGE 213

DID YOU SEE THAT, WEIRD RANDALL?! HA HA HA!
MR. FISHER WAS SO DISTRACTED BY HIS PHONE THAT HE JUST LEFT US! HA HA!
HA
HA
HA
OH—HEY, MR. HARRIS!
?
WHOOOAAA-
SPUD!
SPUD!
-WHOOP!
WHONK!
MR. HARRIS!! ARE YOU OKAY?
HELP MR. HARRIS
GO TO PAGE 116
GO TO CLASS
GO TO PAGE 42

PART 2
Mr Fisher's Wis
A WORD-AND-PICTURE COMIC CARTOON STORY BY MITCH
YOUR WISH HAS BEEN GRANTED
WOW! REALLY?
NO, EGGS CAN'T GIVE WISHES!
HA HA HA
MAD
HA HA HA
MORE FUN ON PAGE 84

GO TO PAGE 196

GO TO PAGE 142

GO TO PAGE 151

GO TO PAGE 191

EASY, TODD—CALM DOWN.
BUT SCOTT'S BEING SO MEAN!

IT'S NOT REAL, TODD—NONE OF THIS IS. REMEMBER?

WHAT DOES THAT EVEN MEAN—

LIFT

THAT WAS ALL VR?!!

THAT WAS SO COOL! IT'S SO LIFELIKE— MEGAN, YOU HAVE TO TRY THIS THING! HA HA!
...IS THAT OLIVIA?
WAIT 'TIL YOU SEE MY DRONE.

A DRONE?! PLEASE TELL ME YOU BROUGHT IT! DRONES ARE SO COOL!
SHH!
GO TO PAGE 1

ARE YOU ALL SEEING THIS?
PRI

WHAT THE
WOW!
BUT THAT'S IMPOSSIBLE!
HOW?!
NT
PRINT
PRINT
PRINT
"SPECIAL MODE"?

MORE! MAKE MORE!
ON IT!
100

HA HA HA HA HA HA HA
PRINT
PRINT
PRINT
PRINT
PRINT

BEST COPY MACHINE EVER!
TRY THIS ONE!
YOMP!
HMMF!
NOM!

HERE—COPY MY POTATOES.

GO TO PAGE 70

I DON'T BELIEVE IT—HE ACTUALLY JUST LET US GO!
YOU SAVED US, WEIRD RANDALL!
HA
HA

...WEIRD RANDALL?
-SNIFF-
I KEEP HIM IN MY EAR—HE'S NOT THERE!

MELVIN'S NEVER BEEN ALONE BEFORE.
IT'S JUST GUM, RIGHT? I BET CHAR-LOTTE HAS SOME.
-SNIFF-

—WE HAVE TO FIND HIM.
ARE YOU... CRYING??
IT'S OKAY—DON'T CRY.

HERE—I'LL HELP YOU FIND YOUR GUM. WE'LL COME BACK FOR THESE.
MELVIN?
OKAY, NOW WE JUST HAVE TO RETRACE YOUR STEPS...
TURN THE PAGE

I liked your project for the science fair. you broke the mold! LOL Also, I saw you at the school talent show.

GO TO PAGE 127

WELL—I'M SORRY, CLASS...
BUT...
WITHOUT A PRINTER, WE CAN'T PRINT OUR NEWSPAPER.
YEAH—NICE GOING, SCOTT!
SHUT UP!!
I'LL SEE IF MR. H CAN REPAIR THE POOR THING. IN THE MEANTIME—EAT THE REST OF THESE DONUTS.
AND SCOTT—
FOLLOW ME TO THE OFFICE.
BUSTED! HA HA!
BUT I DIDN'T DO ANYTHING!
SCOTT! COME BACK!
IT'S NOT MY FAULT!
-SNIFF-
WHAT A WEIRD DAY.
AND A TASTY ONE!
HA HA HA HA HA HA
THE END

CHARLOTTE—DOES YOUR COUSIN KNOW A TYLER SHEPPARD?
I'LL ASK HER.

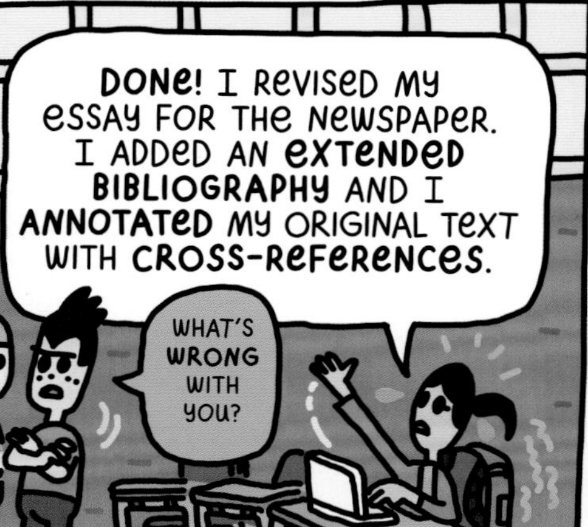
DONE! I REVISED MY ESSAY FOR THE NEWSPAPER. I ADDED AN EXTENDED BIBLIOGRAPHY AND I ANNOTATED MY ORIGINAL TEXT WITH CROSS-REFERENCES.
WHAT'S WRONG WITH YOU?

OKAY, SHE TEXTED BACK.
AND? DOES SHE KNOW MITCH'S PEN PAL? TYLER?

SHE SAYS HER FRIEND KNOWS A GIRL WHO EATS LUNCH WITH SOMEONE WHO IS FRIENDS WITH THE BOYFRIEND OF ONE OF TYLER'S BEST FRIENDS.
WHAT?!
I THINK THAT MEANS YES.

HOLD UP—HE TEXTED.
TYLER? ALREADY?!
WHAT SHOULD WE SAY?

I DON'T KNOW.
MITCH LOVES MOVIES—ASK TYLER IF HE HAS A FAVORITE MOVIE.
GO TO PAGE 38

WHAT WAS THAT?!
I DON'T KNOW! RUN!!

WHOOOOOAAAAA—
SSSSLUDGE

—OOF!!

MEGAN! ARE YOU OKAY?
THUMAAM...

...THE MUCK MAN...

GO TO PAGE 132

GO TO PAGE 136

WHOA. DID SHE JUST—
BANG!
EW!! WHAT IS THIS FILM RATED?!

HEY, LOOK—THEY'RE CROSSING THE THRESHOLD! THEY JUST CROSSED IT!
WHAT? WHAT'S A THRESH-HOLE?

A THRESHOLD IS A CLASSIC PAGE TWENTY-FIVE STORY BEAT—LEAVING THE FAMILIAR TO STEP INTO UNCHARTED WATERS.
YOU'RE RUINING THE MOVIE.

GO TO PAGE 135

HA! I'M DOING IT—I'M WRITING A POEM!
CAN I SEE?
NOT YET! OKAY—WHAT RHYMES WITH DILLON?...
AS A DILLON
TAP TAP
DILLON...DILLON... OH! BILLION!
THAT'S NOT A RHYME!
...GRILLIN'?
GRILLIN'?
GRILLIN'! LIKE, GRILLIN' BURGERS. NO—CHILLIN'!
CHILLIN'?
HE WAS VERY GOOD AT CHILLIN'?
NO.
HMM...VILLAIN!
WHAT?! HE'S NOT A VILLAIN.
DILLON WAS NOT A VILLAIN.
YEAH—SAY THAT.
GO TO PAGE 189

COME ON!
YOU'RE FOLLOWING IT?

UGH...
I CAN'T BELIEVE I'M DOING THIS!

I CAN'T BELIEVE I ACTUALLY SAW IT!!

THE BOYS' LOCKER ROOM IS SO GROSS! EW! WHY COULDN'T IT HAVE GONE SOMEWHERE NOT GROSS?!

IT'S EMPTY... LET'S GO!

UGH...FINE.

GO TO PAGE 40

ANYONE?

SNIFF
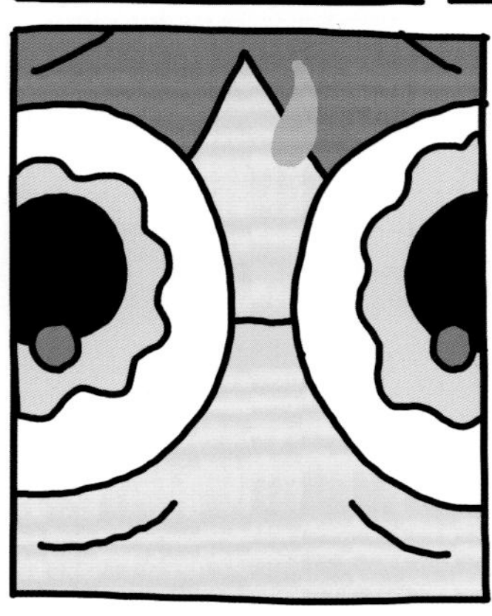

WAUGH!

HA HA! YOU'RE CRYING!!
SCOTT!

HERE—I WILL DO MY HAPPY DANCE FOR YOU.
?
GO TO PAGE 203

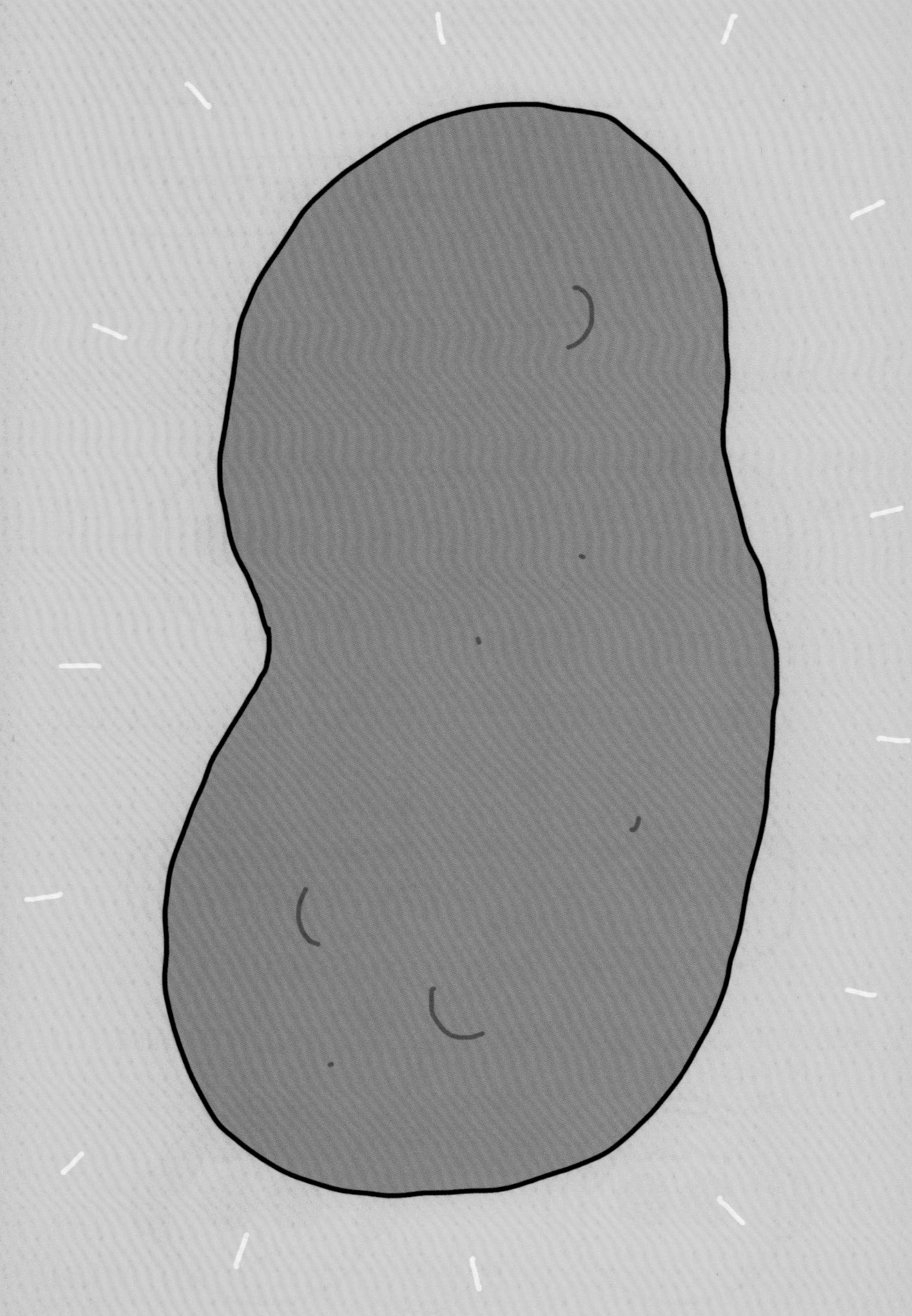

HOW TO DRAW

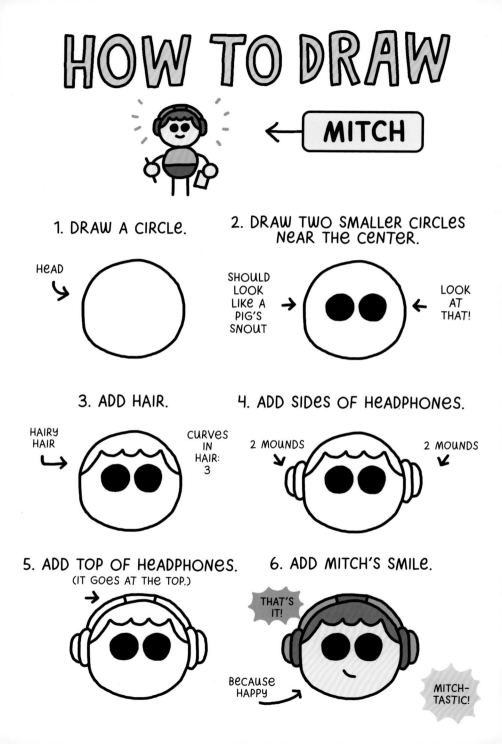

1. DRAW A CIRCLE.

2. DRAW TWO SMALLER CIRCLES NEAR THE CENTER.

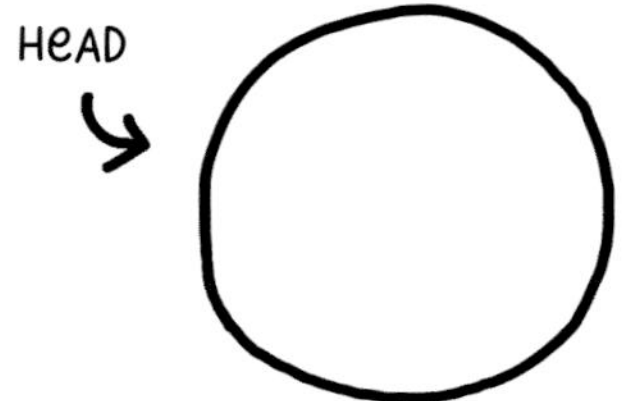

3. ADD HAIR.

4. ADD SIDES OF HEADPHONES.

5. ADD TOP OF HEADPHONES.

(IT GOES AT THE TOP.)

6. ADD MITCH'S SMILE.

HOW TO DRAW

1. DRAW A—**WAIT**. WHAT **DOES** THE MUCK MAN'S HEAD EVEN LOOK LIKE?

2. DOES THE MUCK MAN EVEN **HAVE** EYES?

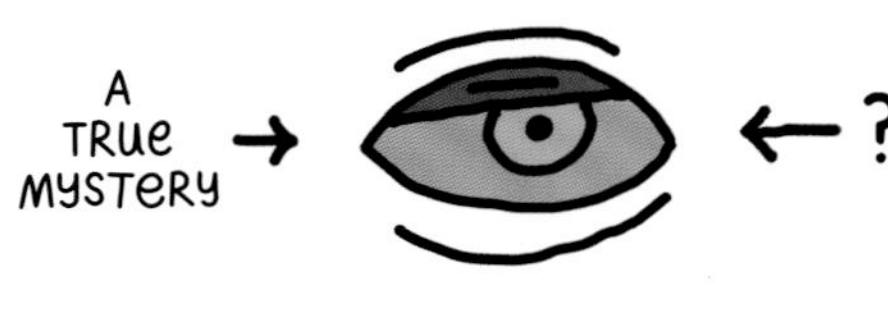

3. AND WHAT DO HIS **TEETH** LOOK LIKE?

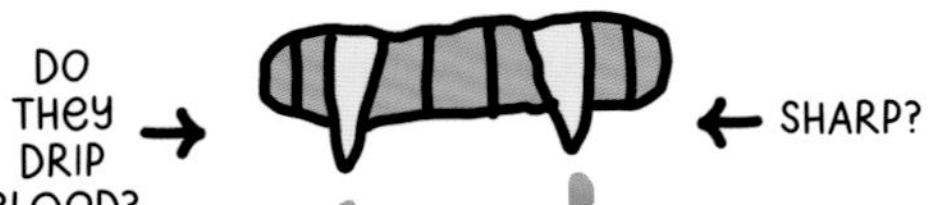

4. DOES HE HAVE FINGERS?

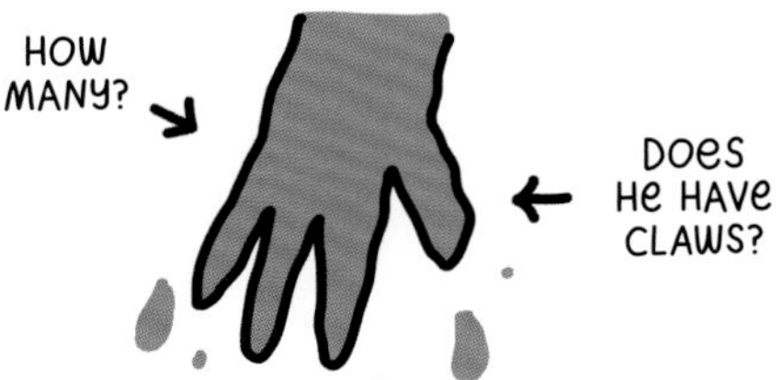

5. SOME HAVE SEEN THE MUCK MAN'S **TRACKS**.

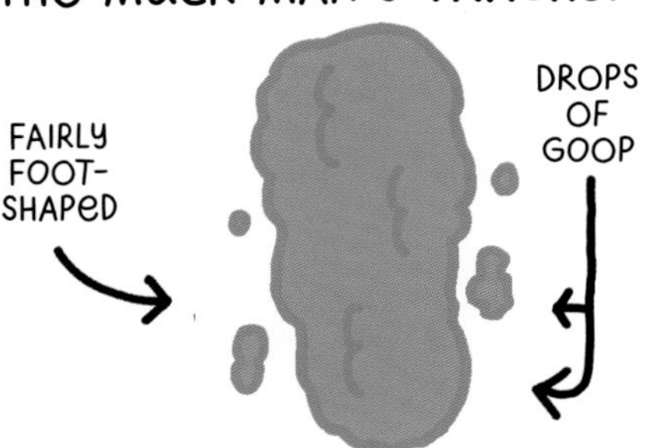

6. WILL WE EVER KNOW WHAT THE MUCK MAN LOOKS LIKE?

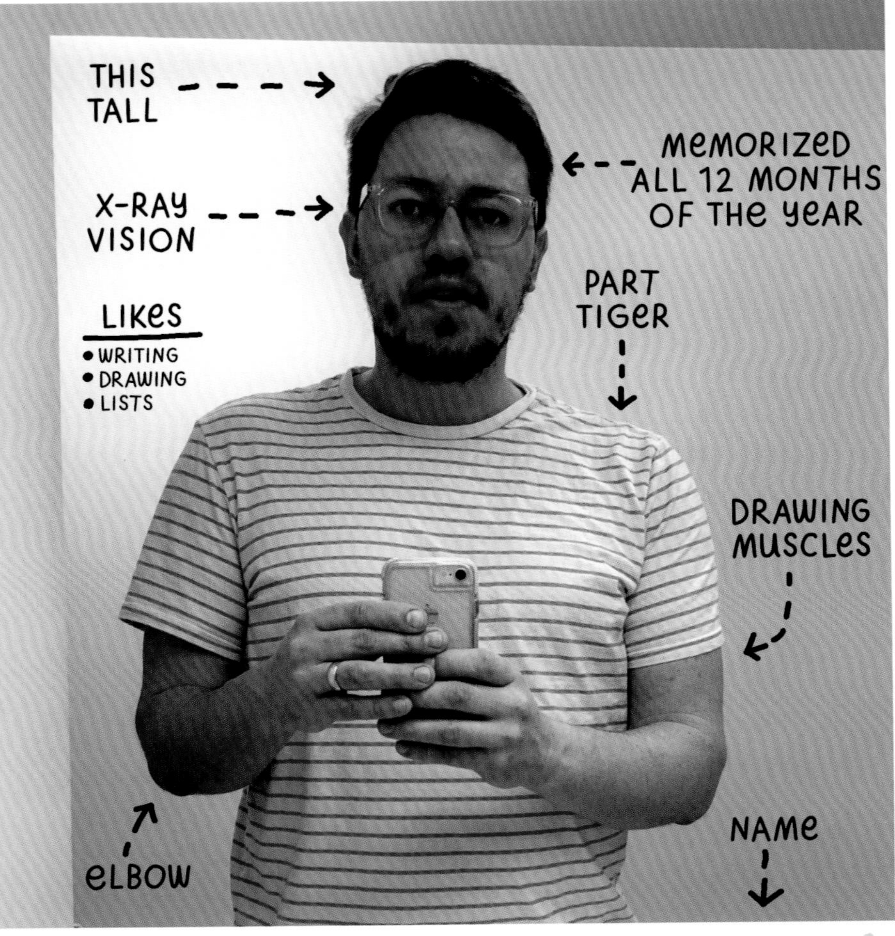

JESS SMART SMILEY

JESS SMART SMILEY IS A JOKE—**SERIOUSLY**.

HE MAKES RAD PICTURES WITH HIS BARE HANDS AND HAS HELPED THOUSANDS OF CHILDREN, TEENS, AND ADULTS AROUND THE WORLD TO CREATE THEIR FIRST COMICS.

JESS IS THE CREATOR OF **LET'S MAKE COMICS!: AN ACTIVITY BOOK TO CREATE, WRITE, AND DRAW YOUR OWN CARTOONS**. HE LOVES SHARING HIS PASSION FOR WRITING, DRAWING, AND STORYTELLING WITH SCHOOLS, LIBRARIES, BOOKSTORES, AND STUDENTS OF ALL AGES AND SKILL LEVELS.

JESS LIVES IN UTAH WITH HIS WIFE AND FOUR CHILDREN.

JESS-SMILEY.COM

THIS BOOK IS FOR A

PUBLISHED BY FIRST SECOND
FIRST SECOND IS AN IMPRINT OF ROARING BROOK PRESS, A DIVISION OF HOLTZBRINCK PUBLISHING HOLDINGS LIMITED PARTNERSHIP
120 BROADWAY, NEW YORK, NY 10271
FIRSTSECONDBOOKS.COM
MACKIDS.COM

LIBRARY OF CONGRESS CONTROL NUMBER: 2023937721

FIRST EDITION, 2024
EDITED BY CALISTA BRILL AND ALEX LU
SERIES DESIGN BY KIRK BENSHOFF
COVER AND INTERIOR BOOK DESIGN BY CASPER MANNING
PRODUCTION EDITING BY DAWN RYAN AND STARR BAER

DRAWINGS CREATED ON IPAD PRO USING AN APPLE PENCIL IN MEDIBANG PAINT PRO. LETTERED AND COLORED DIGITALLY IN PHOTOSHOP.

PRINTED IN CHINA BY RR DONNELLEY ASIA PRINTING SOLUTIONS LTD., DONGGUAN CITY, GUANGDONG PROVINCE

ISBN 978-1-250-89099-3 (PAPERBACK)
10 9 8 7 6 5 4 3 2 1

ISBN 978-1-250-77285-5 (HARDCOVER)
10 9 8 7 6 5 4 3 2 1